Death in a N

By Peter Mckeirnon

The work in this book is fiction. Although place names may be real, characters and events are a product of the author's imagination. Any resemblance to actual events and characters are entirely coincidental. The reproduction of this work in full or part is forbidden without written consent from the author.

ISBN-13: 978-1490935263
ISBN-10: 1490935266

Acknowledgements

Book cover by Grey Lion Design

Original cover image by Heesom Photography

Internal Images Wise Owl Imagery, Paul Leech, Mark Hubbard and Heesom Photography

Youtube Death in a Northern Town trailer by Graham Kirk

For my beautiful wife Kay and my amazing son Alex.

Without your support this would not have been possible.

Undeadications Page

Stephen Fogg, Jo-Anne Burke, Heather Colquhoun, Anthony "Chewy on the Outside" Rosenberg, Charlotte on the Cross, Weeza White, Jenny Shaw, Andy Hayes, Rob "Braaaaaiiins" Kelly, Lisa Edwards, Jane "Best sister-in-law Ever" Goldsmith, Geek, The Big sis ' Mark 1, Simon "Heesom Slayer" Martindale, Dirk McBison-Grinder, Peter Sariwee, Paul "Moose" Turner, Julia "Posh Bird" Kelly, Jordan "Sylar" Turner, Lee Cooper, Jack "Whiskey" Turner, Jean Mckeirnon, Jackie Kinsella, Kerry Edwards, Jason Judge, Amanda Waddell, Jack Price, Lorraine Duckworth, James Edward Yates, Anita Blakey, John McGrath, Gina Noble, Grace Smith, Ashlee Brown, Jenifer Cliffe, Joseph Baxter, Jonathon Yenson, Charley Gerrard, Sam Gerrard, Paul Charters, Jacob Gerrard, Sian Parry, Mal Keenan, Trish Jenkins, Margo Morfield, Tanya Bennison, Lou Butterworth, Mel Simo, Andy Osborne, Charlie Murrell, Andy "Spud" Smith, Michelle Jones, Paul "Jabba" Jowett, Beth "Katsue" Roberts, Ian Hoyles, Dawn Ellis, Kay Mckeirnon, Joseph O'Reilly, Phil Dyke, Carl Yates, Simon 'contributed nothing' Dooley, Hizzle Hozzle, Spud Zombo Mac, Martyn Biggs 'undead extra', Paul Azrael Phoenix, Sue McPherson, Craig Carter, Gary Littlemore, Chris Biggs, Valerie 'Tequila' Shiels, Ann Wolstenholme, Tony Greenhalgh, Amy Baker-Owen, Joanne Aston, Ellie Mae Aston, Melany Brunka, Liam Shaw, Kieron 'Al-suq Yadiq' Taylor, Natasha Cooper, Addison Cooper, Katy Gearing, Gary Walker, Ceris 'Cegsyboo' Breckell, Tom 'Hockey boy'

Robbo, Salli Roberts, Wesley Jones, Helen 'almost dead' Coakley, Bonnie Low, Phil 'almost dead' Humphreys, Mary Lillian 'almost dead' Bennett, Neil Gallagher, Penny Abbott, Sarah 'survives another day' Layton, Hayley 'Hazardous' Moore, Kev Rice, Daniel Ryder, Chris Bignall, Donna Green, Joanne Whitehead, Karen Hay, Tyler Brown ready to survive and die trying, Cal Laurie, Karen Randles, Lizbeth Curbishley, Catherine Wright, Antonia Chandler, Ness Pyatt, Andy Gerrard, Lisa Gerrard, Joanne Bradburne, Mark Curbishley, Tracey Burton, Andre Henri Versluys, Dom Watson, Clare 'stick girl' Sing, Lisa Watson, Teagan Cross, Paige Cross, Ethan Cross, Jack Cross and last but not least my one true love, Phil Brake.

The Beginning

In the early morning of Friday 15th February 2013, reports began to circulate of a meteor resembling a large yellow fireball being spotted in the Russian skies, streaking over the city of Yekaterinburg.

At 09:20 (03:20 GMT), reports confirmed that the meteor had crashed in Russia's Ural Mountains, injuring at least 100 people with much of the impact felt in the city of Chelyabinsk, 200km south of Yekaterinburg.

Reports inform that there were no fatalities and the majority of those affected suffered minor cuts and bruises, with only a few receiving head injuries, and all were being treated at hospital. The proceeding shockwave, caused by the meteors impact, blew out windows and rocked buildings to their core in the neighbouring Chelyabinsk region.

Russian President Vladimir Putin, told reporters that he thanked God that no big fragments had fallen in any populated areas, promising immediate aid for those affected by the incident.

The Russian Emergencies Ministry released a statement informing that thousands of rescue workers had been dispatched to the area to provide help to the injured and to assist with any of the damage caused by the impact.

Russian officials had informed reporters that a large meteor had partially burned up in the planet's lower atmosphere, resulting in the fragments falling to earth.

What they failed to declare to the press was that a large fragment landed in a lake near Chebarkul, a town in the neighbouring Chelyabinsk region, which is home to many factories, a nuclear power plant and more importantly the Mayak atomic waste storage and treatment centre. The lake in question was Lake Karachay, which is, according to the Washington DC based Worldwatch Institute on Atomic Waste, the most polluted place on the planet.

Since 1951, the Russian Government has been using Lake Karachay to discard nuclear waste produced at the nearby Mayak Atomic Waste Storage and Treatment Centre.

The Natural Resources Defense Council produced a report stating that the radiation level of Lake Karachay and its surrounding region has been measured as 600 rontgens per hour. This level of radiation is more than enough to kill a man within 60 minutes of contamination.

Following a drought in the 1960s, Lake Karachay started to dry out and winds carried radioactive dust away from the area, killing a reported half a million people. To prevent such a thing from happening again, the Russian Government filled the lake with over 10,000 hollow concrete blocks in an effort to stop radioactive sediments from shifting. Until now, this had proven to be an effective method and there had been no further incidents.

Until now...

Diary entry 1: Monday 25th February 2013

If you are reading this then lucky you, you made it, you're a survivor. The world went to shit and you made it through to the other side. How is the planet by the way? I hope the putrid smell currently filling my poor cursed nostrils has been eradicated. Not sure how you'd manage that one though. The stench of the dead is a difficult odour to remove. I'm only one day in and the vile smell of death is everywhere. Maybe once you had killed all the dead people, you constructed a giant sprinkler system used to spray Febreeze all over the Earth? Or maybe Flash has become the biggest company on the globe after producing a Vanish Oxi Action tablet specifically designed to wash away the fetid, rotting, air polluting, decaying human corpses that are filling up our streets? Oh man I need to stop thinking about this. My gag reflex has never been great and I've lost count of the times I've thrown up today.

I'd like to think that the human race will triumph, kicking the apocalypse square in its nutsack. As for me, well, if you've found this journal, it probably means I'm dead... or worse.

Well I suppose I best introduce myself. My name is John Diant. I am a 34 year old father of one from a small town in the north of England called Runcorn and before all hell broke loose, I tested mayonnaise for a living. Day in, day out, I did nothing but taste cold, thick mayonnaise for eight hours a day. Even if you like mayonnaise (*which I don't*), a full working day spooning samples of white eggy emulsion into your mouth is too much for anyone. Why would anybody want to taint their food with that muck anyway? Imagine, you've got in front of you a freshly made honey roast ham, cheddar cheese and salad sandwich. Not the pre-packaged rubbish you get from supermarkets but homemade. Perfection on a plate. Who in their right mind thinks *"I know what this delicious sandwich needs. A big fat dollop of salt, egg yolk, oil and vinegar."* The biggest manufacturer in the mayonnaise making business is Hellman's. Well if you ask me, the clue is in the name.

Sorry about that. I just really hate mayonnaise. But I'll try and keep my loathing of the white condiment of the damned to myself from now on.

Well it's been a day now. One day since the life I knew was replaced with the nightmare I've often talked about. The apocalypse and the many forms of how it may arrive had been a favourite topic of mine when the world was a normal place with no fear of it ever actually happening. Growing up, my brother Butty (*I'll get to why he's called that another time - make sure you're not eating anything when I tell you*) and I would spend hours discussing what could happen, what we would do, what weapons we would need, who we would save and where we would go.

Well if I'm honest, it was my brother that would do most of the talking. The guy was, and still is, apocalypse obsessed. A real doom monger. But thinking about it now, if it wasn't for all the meticulous doomsday planning over the years, I probably wouldn't be here now, writing this journal.

So I bet you're wondering how this all began? How, in one day, did I go from being John Diant, father, brother and head of the Anti Mayonnaise Society, to John Diant, father, brother and slayer of the living dead? Well, I'll tell you...

The end of the world began on Monday February 25th and it was my first day back at work after spending a quiet week at home with my daughter Emily for half term. We had a pact that every half term we block out the outside world and spend the whole week with each other. No phones, emails, twitter or Facebook. Just the two of us spending some quality father and daughter time together. Emily, being fifteen, would normally spend all of her free time with her friends doing whatever teenage girls do. Chatting about boy bands and learning dance routines whilst singing into a hairbrush I should imagine. Or rather that's what I like to think she is doing. The reality of what my beautiful, innocent daughter gets up to would probably be too much for my poor addled mind to take and it would no doubt shut down completely. I'm not a prude and I fully understand the world *was* a different place from when I was Emily's age but what father doesn't want their precious little girl to stay a child forever? To not grow up and discover boys? And Sex! Christ on a stick! As far as I'm concerned, Emily will never have sex - it just isn't possible. If she should ever marry (which is *highly unlikely given the current circumstances, as eligible boys that still have a pulse are becoming rarer by the day)* and have children, it will be by Immaculate Conception. My mind cannot process it any other way. But every half term it was just the two of us and they were the happiest times of my life.

I worked in the quality assurance laboratory of a mayonnaise production factory on a once thriving industrial estate called Astmoor, which now housed mostly derelict buildings. It was a sign of the times unfortunately, as businesses on the estate either went bust or moved to more affordable premises. Work was incredibly quiet and, due to the current economic climate, orders for products had suffered resulting in an all time low for the company. Management had responded by letting go of all agency staff so I had anticipated work would be quiet but something wasn't right. We only had one cook on the shop floor when there were usually eight and we didn't have enough staff to run the packaging lines. That meant only one thing.

NO MAYONNAISE TASTING FOR ME!

Normally, I would have been overjoyed to be told we were closing early but this, this was different. There was an eerie silence on the factory floor. It wasn't just down to the missing staff either. Deliveries were not arriving and the surrounding offices and warehouses that were still operational were quiet too. The one manager that made it in to work was Simon Burke, but he really shouldn't have, as his profuse sweating, vile smell, coughing and vomiting were violating more health and safety rules than I care to remember. To be honest, take away the coughing and vomiting and I could have described his appearance on any given day. To say he doesn't look after himself would be an understatement. Have you ever seen the movie Big Trouble in Little China? If you haven't then I apologise as this description will mean nothing to you but there is a guy in the movie that makes himself combust. To do this, he holds his breath and begins to inflate until he explodes. Right before the point of explosion, the man's face is huge and expanded to breaking point. This is what Simon looks like on a daily basis. Like a giant blistered tomato. He is the kind of man that never washes his hands after using the toilet but still needs to wipe them on a towel. The lads in work and I would often joke about what we imagined to be Simon's daily grooming routine. We would joke that he starts his day by rolling out of bed still wearing yesterday's clothes, brush his teeth with a toilet brush then wash his face in his dog's water bowl. Simon, when offered a can of orange soda, once said to me...

"I don't like orange soda, it makes my teeth all slimy..."

Watch out ladies, Simon Burke is hitting the town!

Now, before you start thinking how horrible we all are for talking about our manager this way, I must point out that this guy is a complete dick. His attitude stinks just as much as his breath does. I've known this guy to purposely pay people less than they've earned just because they had rubbed him up the wrong way or disagreed with him about something. Not to mention the tonnes of product that had failed quality checks, only to be later approved by this walking puss bag. This is product that left our factory, was placed on supermarket shelves and then ultimately, ended up in your fridges. Like I said, he's a complete dick!

Stinky puss face, oh sorry, I mean Simon, could not give any explanation as to why work was so quiet or to where everyone was. But still, an early finish from work was not to be sniffed at and neither was puss face, so I didn't hesitate for a second in getting out of there. After 2 hours in the tasting room, which has no windows, no air conditioning and is just about roomy enough to swing a gerbil, I was ready for some fresh air.

I left the tasting room and made my way across the empty factory floor. On a normal day, the factory would be so full of noise generated from packing production lines you could barely hear yourself think. Not on this day. On this day the only sound you could hear was the wind whistling through the holes in the roof. I'm really selling this place to you aren't I? Well don't you worry, should the day come when normality is restored and society has rebuilt, there will always be plenty of jobs available at the mayonnaise factory. I can't see how a new dawn for mankind would remove the fact that this truly is a horrible place to work and I'm sure the high turnover of staff will continue.

I reached the locker room located next to the staff entrance/exit. Unsurprisingly, this room was also empty, except for one person. Stood, placing his work clothes into his open locker, wearing sunglasses (*indoors and in winter might I add*), listening to music through headphones connected to an original Sony Walkman cassette player (*I think he was listening to 'I ran' by Flock of Seagulls but I couldn't be sure*) which was clipped on to his trouser belt loop and with an unlit cigarette hanging out of his mouth was 80s Dave. Now 80s Dave is the same age as me and where I share a nostalgic love for the 1980s, it being the decade of my childhood, Dave is obsessed with this era. 80s movies, 80s music, 80s clothing, 80s gaming - if it happened in the 80s, Dave loves it, and he wants everyone he knows to love it too. I currently have several 80s electro pop mix tapes in my locker that Dave made for me. This is all well and good as I like 80s electro pop as much as the next guy but these mix tapes have been compiled on TDK C90 cassettes. Like most people living in the present, I don't own a cassette player and haven't for many years. Telling him this gets you nowhere however. He simply doesn't understand why a person wouldn't own a cassette player.

Physically, 80s Dave is quite intimidating and with his thick Liverpool accent, he can come across as being abrupt and unapproachable. But if he decides he likes you, he's a good friend, even if he does bang on about his love for Gary Numan and all things electro pop every five minutes.

The other nickname bequeathed to him by work colleagues is Dump Truck. He was given the name Dump Truck due to his size and stocky build. Also, using the toilet directly after him is something you want to avoid at all costs. I've seen a lot since the world went tits up and I can honestly say, I would rather share a room with a rotting flesh torn, maggot infested corpse than be anywhere near the vicinity of a toilet Dave has just used to take a shit.

"Alright kidda, you walking up?" he said, placing the last of his work gear into his locker.

Dave was born and raised in Liverpool, which is no more than at thirty minute drive from Runcorn. Now if you are not familiar with the 'Scouse' accent it is heavily influenced by the large number of immigrants that have settled in Liverpool over the years. Some from Scotland and the Isle of Man but mostly from Ireland. The accent is fast paced and unlike any other dialect you will find in the UK due to its unique speech patterns. As a quick guide, you may find the following 'Scouse' slang interpretations useful.

11

"Lar" – often used to start or end a sentence when referring to or having a conversation with a friend. *"Lad"* may also be used.

"Kidda" or *"Ace"* – also used to refer to a friend but more often than not, saved for use with a close friend.

"Ad Off" – Used when someone has ripped you off or stolen something from you. *"He ad off with my bike!"* Also used when losing an argument.

"Go ed" – *"Go ahead"* or *"Go on."*

"Arl Arse" - When someone has done something cruel or mean spirited. *"Stop being such an arl arse!"*

Those are the basics and the words 80s Dave likes to use most commonly. He's also heavily into swearing, so please accept my apologies for any language used in this journal that might offend. In fact, no, fuck it. It's the end of the world. If ever there was a time for swearing then that twatting time, is now!

"Hiya Dave," I responded, *"Yes mate I'm walking up. Let's hurry up and get out of here before Simon changes his mind and keeps the place open."*

"Doubt it lar, have you seen the kip of him? He looks like the world is about to fall out of his arse. Fucking hilarious. Speaking of which, I'm just going for a quick dumpski. Saves using my own bog paper when I get home. I only ever take a crap on work time. I'm so good at it now I

haven't bought any toilet paper for six months. I can even hold one in all weekend. Two days straight lar. My sphincter is the strongest muscle in my body kidda. Hey, I can close my arsehole so fast it can double up as a cigar cutter! Wait for me outside daddy 'O'."

"Gladly Dave," I said, "I might even start walking up slowly, the further away from you and that toilet I am the better."

"There's no need for that lar. My shit smells like I look. Fucking sweet! I'll see you outside Ace," and with that, Dave left the locker room.

I finished up in the locker room, clocked out and exited the factory. It was a cool and crisp winter morning. The sky was clear and the sun was shining but it was cold, most definitely below zero, and I was eager to start my walk home.

I waited outside the staff entrance for Dump Truck to finish unloading his cargo. I took out my phone to text Emily to let her know I had finished work and I was going to be home when she got in from school. It's always best to let your kids know if you're going to be home early. It saves any unnecessary embarrassment on both sides.

No signal.

Now it isn't uncommon for mobile phone signals in Runcorn to be erratic. I've often surmised that the reason for the terrible reception in Runcorn is because it is an industrial town with a chemical manufacturing plant situated at the heart. I've conversed on many occasions that the surrounding thick smog of chemicals that encase the town is responsible for stopping any signal from getting in or out. I also think it's the reason every other person here needs an inhaler but hey, I'm no doctor so what do I know?

I decided to walk around the outside of the factory to see if it would help to gain a phone signal. Knowing how long it normally takes Dave when he visits the lavatory, I knew I'd have plenty of time before he made an appearance. There is a small path at the side of the factory that takes you through to the back entrance and to where the staff car park is situated. As I walked along the path, phone in hand with my arm raised in the air (*because when you can't get a phone signal, holding it aloft with your arm outstretched will surely resolve the problem*) I noticed a lone starling flying into my line of sight. Now, I'm no 'Twitcher', but I do know that starlings are highly social birds and are often seen flying in flocks called a murmuration, so seeing one on its own was not common place.

Hang on, how the hell do I know that? Maybe I am a secret bird watcher after all. Well who would have thought it? Even after the end of the world you can learn something new about yourself. It's typical that I've just found out I could have a new hobby and it is now practically obsolete. I don't fancy the chances of anyone nuts enough to venture outside hoping to catch a rare glimpse of the once common chaffinch. Bird watching would be classed as an extreme sport these days and you'd have to be a great tit to try it (*see what I did there?*).

Starlings are common place in this town. Normally I wouldn't give one of the little fellas a second glance but something about this bird and how it was flying caught my attention. Its flight was irregular and without direction. It looked increasingly like the starling was struggling to fly and it kept dropping in height. It would flap its wings, fall, flap its wings and fall again. This continued and I watched as the bird flew towards my location, continuing to drop until it ceased flying all together, landing not 10ft away from me.

As I walked towards the starling, my heart began to pound so fast and so hard I could feel it through my chest. Seeing this bird fall from the sky had really spooked me and I became overwhelmed with feelings of unease. Saliva filled my mouth and my stomach began to churn. For me, this is a precursor to vomiting and as I mentioned earlier, I don't have the best gag reflex in the world. Just the thought of what I was possibly going to see was enough to make me feel sick. I reached the bird and hesitantly checked over it. It was still alive but only barely. The fall had broken one of the starling's legs which had snapped so severely, it resembled a broken twig. Its left wing was almost torn completely from its body and it lay, quietly twitching, in a bed of feathers and blood. As I watched the bird take its last laboured breath, I swear that it was looking at me, and with resignation in its eyes, I watched it die.

Thud!

"What the fuck was that?" I said as I heard the sound of something hitting the ground.

Thud!

There it was again, only this time closer than the last. I looked behind me to see that lying dead on the ground was another starling and beyond that was another.

I reached again for my phone, with the only thought in my mind being contact Emily. I couldn't quite place it but I had a feeling that something was seriously wrong and all I wanted to do was to speak to my daughter.

Still no signal.

With phone in hand, I raised my arm in the air once again in a vain attempt to gain a signal. In the sky directly in front of me was a small murmuration of starlings. One by one I watched as they fell from the sky. For one surreal moment I imagined my life had become a Hitchcock movie because as terrifying as this was, nothing about what I was witnessing seemed real. How could it?

Thud!

Another starling dead.

Thud!

And another.

More and more birds began to fall all around me and I had no idea what to do. I crouched down, pulling my coat over my head, hoping that one wouldn't hit me.

Silence.

The sounds of birds falling to their death had stopped. I stood up straight, removed the coat from over my head and slowly opened my eyes. It was a massacre. Birds lay dead all around me. What the hell just happened? I had never seen or heard of anything like this in my life. Were they poisoned? Was it a mass suicide? My head began to hurt as I tried to comprehend what I had witnessed. Then I heard it again.

Thud!

Only this time it was followed by a car alarm coming from the staff car park. I walked, carefully navigating my steps around the dead birds that lay on the path till I could see the car park in front of me. A starling had fallen and landed on the roof of Stinky Puss face's, sorry, force of habit, Simon car. The dirt bag himself was leaning again his car door, coughing and holding his stomach whilst trying to put his key in the lock.

"Fuck me lar, have you seen all those dead birds back there?" said 80s Dave as he walked up behind me, headphones and sunglasses on with cigarette in mouth.

Unable to find words, I looked at Dave and nodded towards Simon. Dave walked past me to see what I was nodding at. Unsurprisingly, he took delight in what stood before him and wasn't going to miss an opportunity to annoy his boss.

"Hey Simon! Do you know you've got a dead bird splattered on top of your car?" he shouted, a slight smirk on his face as he puffed on his cigarette.

Simon looked over to Dave and stared at him for a few seconds but did not respond. Instead, body shaking, he returned to the task at hand and attempted to put his key in the car door. Jittering uncontrollably, he dropped the keys under the front right wheel of the vehicle. As he got down on his knees, Simon grabbed his stomach again and screamed in pain.

"I think he's getting worse Dave, we can't just stand here doing nothing, why don't you go and give him a hand? I'll stay here and try and get a phone signal. If I do, I'll call for an ambulance," I said, knowing very well that his response would be anything but forthcoming.

"No chance mate, look at the state of him. He always looks like shit but never this bad. I'm not catching whatever the

hell kind of illness he's got. You go," came the expected reply.

Before I could respond, Simon lent forward and holding his stomach, was violently sick. Have you watched The Exorcist? If you have you'll know what scene I'm talking about. Well that was child's play compared to what Dave and I were witnessing. It just kept coming and coming and coming. It wasn't just the amount of vomit that was shocking but its colour too. At first it was dark brown, then it was light purple followed by a deep red then it was a mixture of all the colours together. If Hell had rainbows, then they would be the same colour as Simon's puke. Upon seeing this, my mouth once again began to fill with saliva. I swallowed it back down in an attempt to stop the inevitable but it was a futile attempt at best and I threw up all over a dead starling. Dave began to laugh.

"It's not a competition," he said, turning his head to inspect my creation, *"It's quite artistic really. The way you've thrown up all over that dead starling. It makes it difficult to tell what bits came from you and what belongs to the bird. Shame this isn't an art gallery, some ponce would pay good money for that."*

Finally, Simon stopped being sick and quietly knelt there, next to his car, motionless, in a large puddle of puke.

"Looks like he's over the worst of it," I said, wiping a small sliver of bile from my chin.

19

It was then that Simon lost control of all bodily functions and shat himself. There was nothing he could do to stop it. He lent forward, grabbing his stomach again, in a hopeless attempt to halt the mass exodus of turd. Now Dave and I were stood a good 30 feet away from where Simon was kneeling and even we could hear the evacuation that was underway in his trousers, so you can understand how severe this was. He looked across to Dave and I with resignation in his eyes. A look that simply said *"I'm spent, I have nothing left"*. For Dave this was hilarious and he began to belly laugh uncontrollably.

After a few horrific minutes, Simon's anal Hiroshima finally ended. The man looked empty, internally and of mind. What colour he *did* have left, had drained almost completely from his face. Simon, who as mentioned, usually resembled a blistered tomato, now looked almost translucent as he closed his eyes and fell forward, face down in a puddle of his own vomit.

"Bravo!" shouted Dave, applauding the horror show we had just witnessed. Simon didn't move.

"As much as I'd rather ignore everything we've just seen and go home, we're going to have to help him or he's probably going to drown" I said, weaving my way around the fallen starlings as I walked towards the vomit pool where Simon lay.

"Oh alright then, but I'm not touching him, you can do all the hands on work," Dave replied, wiping away tears of laughter. *"I know I said my arsehole is the strongest muscle in my body but even I might struggle to not shit myself if I catch what he's got."*

When we got to Simon it wasn't a pretty sight. His body was either covered in excrement or vomit or both. And the smell! Have you ever smelt something so bad you could taste it? What am I saying, of course you have. If you've survived long enough to read this journal then your nostrils must have been subjected to smells capable of making your nose bleed. There was a small patch of skin on the back of his neck that had not been tainted by shit or sick, but there was a giant boil there, with a big yellow puss filled head just waiting to burst. That's Simon for you!

Both Dave and I stood for a moment looking at the mess lying in front of us, neither wanting to touch him.

"Go on then," I said, gesturing to Dave to turn Simon over, removing his face from the puke puddle.

"OK," he replied, lighting another cigarette.

"Really?" was my surprised response.

"Fuck that lar, you do it," came Dave's real answer.

"No way, you should do it. Just see it as an apology for laughing when he shit himself," I said.

"Come on that was pretty funny lad. This smell isn't though. It probably wouldn't be too bad if it was just the stink of shit and sick, but mix that in with his normal everyday pong and it could strip paint. It's burning my eyes kidda. If I was to remove these sunglasses you'd see two burnt out holes were my irises used to be. And that's coming from a man who smokes 80 a day without hardly any sense of smell or taste! No, you should do it. You like him more than I do." Dave reasoned.

"I like everyone more than you do." I replied.

"Fair point," he replied.

Then suddenly, Simon raised his head out of the vomit, arching his back so that his body from the waist up was lifted off the ground. The way his torso was positioned was unnatural. The human body is not meant to bend that way and it reminded me of a venomous snake preparing itself to strike.

Simon stared straight ahead and with mouth open, let out a lengthy exhale before collapsing back into the vomit. Simon's breathing reminded me of the sound gas makes when you turn on your oven hob before lighting it and, because of the cold weather, you could see his breath, making him look like a human steam pipe.

"Interesting," said Dave as he puffed away on his cigarette, flicking ash on to the back of Simon's once again lifeless

body. My thought's lay with getting help and I turned again to my mobile phone but still no signal.

"Do you think he's dead?" I asked, fearing the worst and with no idea of what we would do if he was.

Dave placed his foot on Simon's back and rocked him back and forth.

"Oi Simon!" he shouted as his foot prodding continued.

Stinky Puss Face did not respond.

"Yep!" was Dave's professional analysis, scraping the bottom of his boot on the ground in an attempt to remove any cross contamination from Simon's body.

"Wow, impressive examination Dr Dave," I said sarcastically.

"Alright smart arse you fucking have a go," came the expected response.

Hesitantly, I knelt down next to Simon, being extremely careful to avoid any contact. But it was no good, to check if he was alive or not I would have to touch him. This would have been an arduous task under normal circumstances but given his current condition, I found it extremely difficult. I reached out my hand and placed my fingers on his neck to check for a pulse. My fingers started to slip and slide as they sunk beneath the thick layer of puke and sweat that coated his skin.

"Aw man, this is disgusting," I squirmed, using everything I had to keep the remaining content of my stomach in my stomach.

"Is he dead or what?" Dave asked, ejecting a cassette from his Walkman, and changing tape sides.

"I can't get a proper grip on his neck to check, my fingers keep slipping. I could do with a scraper or scoop or something to get this gunk off," I said.

Dave looked around at our surroundings. You could see the seeds of an idea start to grow.

"I've thought of something, don't go anywhere, I'll be right back," he said, flicking his cigarette butt into the barf lake then jogging to the back entrance of the factory.

With Dave away and Simon busy breaking the world record for holding your breath whilst face down in sick, I took a moment to think about what the hell had just happened. I scanned my surroundings and counted at least 25 starlings splattered on the ground and that was only what I could see. Sorry, 26. I forgot about the one that landed on top of Simon's car. God knows what it was like further afield. My mind ran wild with images of streets, housing estates and fields all covered in feathered death, birds smashing into cars on roads and motorways causing crashes and accidents, even fatalities.

Then there was Simon. What the fuck had just happened to him? I've seen illness and I've been ill *(there was that time in 97' when I had to keep toilet roll in the fridge. That story is for another time however. This is gross enough, I don't want to make it worse!)* but I have never known anything so severe. Is he dead? Quite possibly. I couldn't find a pulse but then again I'm not a doctor, and it's not like I tried very hard really. Hey don't judge me, I see you tutting and shaking your head. I know I could have done more than just stand around watching him be violently ill. At least I didn't laugh so hard I nearly gave myself a hernia like Dave. You try touching someone covered with a thick layer of goo made from turds, sweat and bile.

Dave emerged from the factory, jogging back over to me and the almost definitely dead Simon. He was carrying what I can only describe as a cross between a 6ft plastic rowing oar, a shovel and a spoon. Kind of like a massive paddle. It was an odd looking piece of equipment and one that the cooks in the factory would use to scoop ingredients from barrels into massive caldrons used to make mayonnaise. The paddle was white of colour, tall with a rounded shovel head and made of hard plastic.

"I'm back," proclaimed Dave, slightly out of breath and lighting up another cigarette as if inhaling the chemicals and nicotine would restore his body back to normal after his little physical exertion. *"You'd have thought Simon*

would have locked up the factory after he left. Suppose he had other things on his mind. Like not shitting his pants."

"What's that thing for?" I asked inquisitively.

"For making mayonnaise," came the perplexed response.

"I know that, I meant what have you brought it over for?" I replied.

For an intelligent man, Dave often completely misses the point of a question or conversation.

"Oh right!" Dave's brain finally switching in to gear, *"For this..."*

He placed the shovel end of the paddle under Simon's torso and pulled the handle down towards the ground, flinging him over onto his back. There was a horrible squelch from the shit in Simon's pants as it squashed against the cold concrete floor before spraying out at either side of his trousers. Simon lay there, eyes closed and mouth open, motionless, with arms spread out. He looked like an angel only with wings made of poo.

"There you go lar, you can check if he's breathing and you don't have to touch him, just put your ear to his mouth and see if you can hear anything," said Dave as he stood looking proud of himself; smoke in one hand and paddle in the other.

"It's amazing the way your mind works," I said.

"Thanks," Dave said, puffing on his fag and then once again flicking ash onto Simon.

"It wasn't a compliment," I replied.

"Well I would have kicked him onto his back but I didn't want to get any shit on my boots," he responded.

"You know Dave, I've never really regarded you as an overly caring and considerate person before but seeing you here now, with Simon, I've come to realise, I'm right, you really couldn't give a monkeys what happens to him could you?"

Dave removed his sun glasses. He meant business.

"No John, I couldn't give a shit. Remember this is the arl arse that still owes me money from working overtime for the last 7 weekends. Every week I get my wage slip and it's flat rate only, no overtime. He keeps saying he'll sort it but the petty little prick never does and do you know why? All because I asked him if he had been burnt as a child and if that was why his face looks like melted cheese."

I looked at Simon, taking a closer inspection of his face.

"You're right, his face does look like melted cheese. More of a blue cheese dressing at the moment but I can see what you mean. Look Dave, I know old stinky here has his faults but we need to put that to one side. I mean, what are we going to do if he's dead? I've been trying and I can't get a phone signal at all so I can't ring for an ambulance. The

network must be down or something and it wouldn't be right to just leave him here. I really want to call Emily too. I can't quite put my finger on it but something about all this isn't right. I don't suppose you've got a mobile phone or are you continuing to deny the last 25 years even happened and it's still 1988?" I asked.

"Hey don't knock it kidda," he replied, replacing his sun glasses, *"It was a good year 1988. It's the year that brought us some of the greatest movies of all time. Beetlejuice, written and directed by Tim Burton, jointly produced by Geffen and Warner Brothers, starring Michael Keaton in the title role with support from Geena Davies and Alec Baldwin. Die Hard written by Steve De Souza, directed by John McTiernan, starring Bruce Willis as New York super cop John McClane. But, by far the greatest film to be released that year was My Neighbour Totoro.'* Dave started to sing. *'Totoro, to-to-ro. Totoro, to-to-ro! Awesome lad."*

"My Neighbour Totoro? Isn't that a cartoon about witches and goblins that live in the woods with people that turn into animals? That's awful mate, a terrible film." I replied.

Dave was clearly getting annoyed with my complete dismissal of My Neighbour Totoro but honestly, it's rubbish. To get his own back, he hit me right in the Keira Knightley's. *"What do you know? You cry every time you watch Love Actually."*

Now it was my turn to see red.

"Love Actually is a bloody good movie I'll have you know. It's an emotional roller-coaster that film and I challenge anyone not to be moved by it. Love Actually explores a level of emotion most modern films fail to touch upon and should be in everyone's top ten list," I argued.

"Shit list," Dave replied, dismissing my argument.

He was loving this now and I'm ashamed to say, we had both completely forgotten about Simon who was still lying motionless and almost certainly dead. Not my proudest moment but that's what happens when I'm challenged on the merits of one of the greatest movies of all time. That's Love Actually by the way, not My Neighbour Totoro, which is rubbish.

"It's anything with Hugh Grant in it for you isn't it? You've got a proper little man crush on him," Dave added.

"Hugh Grant is a brilliant actor," I proclaimed, *"He's versatile, likeable, has amazing hair and is at his best in Love Actually, where he successfully portrays a bumbling Prime Minister looking for love."*

"Substitute Prime Minister for snooty Englishman and you've just described every film he's been in," Dave smirked sucking down the end of another cigarette.

"I have not described every film he's been in. His hair is different in Notting Hill."

29

I was quite proud of that reply at the time but looking back it was probably one of the wankiest things I've ever said.

"How are we friends?" was Dave's response, looking like he was honestly contemplating this.

"Because I'm one of the few that humour your obsession with all things 1980's, that's why. So have you got a mobile or what?"

"Yes I have" Dave replied rather smugly.

I was genuinely surprised by this. Dave with modern technology? Surely not!

"Can I borrow it then?" I asked.

"Well, I don't keep it on me it's too heavy," he replied.

"Too heavy?" My suspicion growing by the second.

"Yeah it comes with its own briefcase because the battery is so big" Dave explained.

I shouldn't have been surprised by this, but I was. He's not called 80s Dave for nothing. It makes perfect sense that his mobile phone would be one of the very first released.

Both Dave and I looked at each other and burst into laughter. Me because of how ridiculous it is to think that he has a mobile phone that needs its own briefcase. Dave was laughing because, well, he either agrees with this sentiment or he's having me on. You can never tell with Dave.

"How long does the battery last?" I asked, struggling to compose myself.

"About forty minutes," came the reply.

Well that was me gone. Laughter took complete control and I no longer had the ability to govern my own actions. If you've ever had a laughing fit take hold of you then you know exactly what I mean. Tears streamed from my eyes, blurring my vision. My laughter became such that I produced no noise. I just stood there, mouth open, shoulders jiggling up and down, eyes closed with tears rolling down my face. I opened my eyes but I could barely see through the glaze of salty liquid that coated my sight. I could just about make out Dave's shape as he lent forward holding his ribs with one hand and steadying himself with the giant paddle in his other. I could hear that he was laughing hysterically. I blinked then wiped my eyes which helped slightly as I could now see that Dave, although a complete giggling mess, was attempting to light another cigarette. I blinked and wiped my eyes again. My vision was almost clear now. I looked at Dave who was still laughing and puffing on a smoke at the same time *(this guy could light up during a hurricane I swear)*. I wish that was all I saw. Behind Dave, stood Simon. Well, what used to be Simon. His eyes were white and sunken, his skin tone almost see-through giving a clear view of the veins running

31

beneath his vomit stained flesh. Simon stood lob sided, as if something heavy was weighing down the left side of his body. This gave the impression that his right shoulder was higher than the left. I remember thinking to myself at the time *'How the fuck is he alive?'* He had just spent the last 10 minutes face down drowning in his own bile, he shouldn't be breathing let alone standing. Dave noticed that I was no longer looking at him but looking past him with my face, wearing a joint expression of confusion and surprise. Dave's laughter began to subside as he realised something had caught my attention and he gave me a look that asked what's wrong. I nodded gesturing for him to turn around and look behind him. He turned and was now face to face with the manager formally known as Simon.

This Shit Just Got Real!

Gleavey was cold. Having misplaced his keys, he had been banging on the door to his house for what felt like an eternity, hoping the noise would wake his partner Ros from her slumber so she could let him in. So far, it hadn't worked.

It was 4am and Dave Gleavey was drunk. His band, Cottonmouth, had been celebrating a triumphant gig at the Albert on Lark Lane, Aigburth, Merseyside the night before. A triumphant gig for Gleavey meant that people turned up to listen to Cottonmouth's own unique brand of stoner metal. Any gig with an audience was reason to celebrate and he needed little excuse to toast a gig.

"Ros, open the fucking door will you?" he shouted through the letterbox, desperate to get inside.

His eagerness for Ros to open the door was not due to how cold he was. Gleavey had once spent a whole winter's night upside down with his foot stuck in a wire fence he had drunkenly tried and failed to climb over. He had been hanging in that fence for so long he lost all feeling in the lower half of his body. Luckily for him, a dog walker found him and called an ambulance. After living through that, cold he could handle. The reason for his keenness to get inside was due to him being desperate to take a shit.

"Come on Ros I'm fucking dying here. I can't hold it in for much longer. What do you want me to do? Crap on the doorstep?" he yelled again through his letterbox.

Dave Gleavey and Rosalind Arden lived together in a terraced house on Dukesfield, a Runcorn housing estate situated close to the Silver Jubilee Bridge or Runcorn Bridge as it was more commonly known. The bridge crossed the river Mersey, connecting the neighbouring towns of Runcorn and Widnes. The houses in Dukefield were old and some still had outside toilets in the back gardens and yards. Not their house though. Theirs had been converted into a brick storage area many years ago. Historically, Gleavey had been using it to store tools, until recently when he had electricity installed. Now he used it to grow 'herbal' remedies.

Next door to them, lived a hard of hearing elderly couple, which was just as well given the late night jamming sessions Cottonmouth would hold on a regular basis. Their outside toilet however, was still in use and if he could scale their garden wall, he could leave a deposit.

Gleavey's arse began to grumble, releasing a growling sound to rival that of a Rottweiler. He was frozen to the spot, poo pains stabbing into his bowels. He dared not risk a movement, fearing the friction produced would result in his pulsating anus liberating the contained load.

After several teeth grinding minutes, the pain began to ease and he felt confident enough to move. He scurried, buttocks clenched together, to the wall separating his neighbours back garden from the cobbled path outside. He thought that if he could scale the wall then maybe, just maybe, his neighbours would had left the door to their outside toilet unlocked and he could finally relieve himself. The wall was over 6ft and Gleavey, being tall himself, would not normally have any problem climbing it but given his intoxicated state, he knew it was going to be a struggle. He attempted a run and jump, only he forgot to jump and instead ploughed face first into the wall; the impact tearing the skin from his forehead.

"Fucking hell!" he yelled, using the sleeve of his jacket to wipe away the warm sticky blood that was oozing from his head.

He tried again, this time remembering to jump. He successfully climbed the wall and straddled the top, legs dangling on either side. He reached inside his jacket and pulled out a six skinner joint.

"Don't mind if I do" he said, lighting the spliff and inhaling deeply.

He tilted his head back and gazed at the cold winter night's sky. The moon was particularly large that night and the sky full of stars. Looking up he pondered the thought that he could have been anywhere. He pulled hard again on his joint. It was good shit but of course it was. He had grown it himself and home grown was always better than anything you could buy from a local dealer. As he looked up, the rest of the world began to melt away. He imagined he was a cowboy and the wall he was straddling was his horse.

Gleavey had always wanted to be a cowboy and for a brief moment, as the marijuana took hold, he indulged in his fantasy and began to hum the theme to Bonanza.

"Dum dada dum dada dum dada dum dada daa daa,"

"Dum dada dum dada dum dada dum, dum dada dum dum dum..." he sang whilst riding the wall like a bucking bronco.

It was a nearby squelching sound that brought him back to reality. He stubbed out the joint on his neighbours wall and placed it back in his jacket pocket. From his position, he could see into all of the gardens attached to the terraced row. Three houses up from his, was Lisa Franey's home. Lisa was a good friend to Roz and Gleavey and they had known each other for many years. From his elevated position he noticed a stooped figure in Lisa's garden but it was too dark for him to make out who or what it was. He strained his intoxicated eyes; looking towards Lisa's garden. Was it his friend or an intruder?

"Lisa, is that you?" he called out, taking a punt on it being his friend and if not, hoping his voice would startle the stooped figure and they would run away.

The stooped figure slowly began to straighten their posture. The movement triggered a motion sensor security light in Lisa's garden; flooding the area with light and blinding his vision. He quickly lifted his hands over his face, shielding his eyes from the sudden influx of light and in doing so lost his balance and almost fell from the wall. As his eyes started to adjust, he lowered his hands and again looked towards Lisa's garden and what he saw chilled him to his core.

The figure in the garden was indeed his friend Lisa, only something horrible had happened to her. Her once tanned skin now appeared grey in colour and her eyes were covered in a white glaze. Blood dripped freely from her mouth and, in her arms, she held the remains of her dead cat, Wilf. On first glance, he had thought Wilf had been in an accident, as he watched steam lift from its blood coated fur, the cat's guts hanging from its torn stomach, glistening in the brightness of the security light. Then to both his surprise and disgust; Lisa buried her head into the cats open chest cavity, greedily chewing on its innards.

"What the fuck...?" he gasped.

The sight of Lisa ravenously devouring her cat was too much for him to process and he began to think smoking that last joint was not one of his better ideas. Then the security light went out and his vision turned to black, his eyes struggling to adjust from the stark contrast of light and dark. He strained his eyes, needing to be sure that what he saw *was* only his mind playing tricks. Reaching down to remove the boot from his foot he threw it towards the garden. The boot triggered the security light again and brightness once more invaded his sight. His eyes adjusted quicker this time but when he looked towards

38

the garden, Lisa was gone and there was not a trace of her cat either. He removed the joint from his jacket pocket and studied it in his hand.

"That is some strong shit," he said, before tossing the joint to the ground.

Gleavey's bottom began to grumble once more; his supposed hallucination distracting him from his urgent need to empty his bowels. He climbed down from the wall into his neighbour's garden and scurried to the door of the outside toilet. The moment of truth. Should the door be locked then all his efforts were to be for nothing. If it was open, he could finally find relief. The Poo Gods had answered his prayers because when he pulled on the handle, the door opened and to his delight, the latrine was fully stocked with toilet paper.

He rushed in, closed the door and instantly found himself in a race with his anus. Could he drop his trousers and place his bottom on the cold plastic seat before his sphincter muscle finally gave way? He could but only just, and with it brought relief at long last. The pain left him instantly in one quick flurry and after hours of agony he was now in complete bliss. The combination of alcohol, marijuana and newly emptied bowels filled him with elation. So much so, he was considering waking his elderly neighbours so he could kiss them for still having an outside toilet, leaving the door unlocked and for keeping it fully stocked with toilet paper.

Now empty, he was ready to clean. He ripped three sheets of toilet paper and folded them ready to wipe. As he lifted his bottom from the cold seat, his knees knocked the toilet door; creaking it open to reveal the undead Lisa, salivating over her would be prey and watching as it wiped its arse.

"Oh shit!" were to be Gleavey's last words, said simultaneously as his index finger on the hand wiping his bottom ripped through the toilet paper and slid into his anus while his undead friend lunged forward, frantically tearing into his flesh.

Journal Entry 2

There they stood, eye balling each other for a few seconds. Then 80s Dave decided to break the silence.

"You look different Simon. Have you changed your hair?"

Simon slowly opened his jaw, strands of thick saliva protruding from top lip to bottom. A noise like nothing I have ever heard a human larynx make before bellowed from his mouth and with it came a smell so bad you could taste it, and it tasted like death. Dave took the full force of Simon's death breath in the face but it didn't seem to bother him. That's the beauty of smoking 80 fags a day you see. It numbs the senses. He waited for Simon to finish roaring at him, then casually took a puff on his cigarette and blew the smoke in his face. Simon again snapped his slobber dripping mouth open then lunged forward at Dave in what looked like an attempt to bite his face. Simon's arms were reaching out and grabbing at Dave wildly but luckily for my retro friend, co-ordination was no longer a skill that Puss Face possessed.

"Fuck me lar!" yelled Dave as he side stepped Simon's blundering attempts to grab him.

It was quite a sight to behold. Simon would lunge at Dave, biting the air and snatching at him madly and then Dave would side step to the right, moving out of the way. It would then take Simon a good few seconds to realise where Dave had moved to and the whole merry dance would start again. After a few minutes of this, Dave started to get bored. Simon on the other hand was relentless in his need to land his catch and looked like he could do this for an eternity.

"Has he lost his marbles or what?" Dave asked.

"He looks like he's trying to eat you!" I replied.

"He can fucking try! I'll rip his face off!" said Dave, side stepping the latest of Simon's advances.

"Look Simon, if this is about me saying your face looks like melted cheese or for laughing when you shat yourself then I'm sorry, there's no need to go all Hannibal Lector on me," he added.

Simon turned to Dave and grabbed at him again.

"Right that's it lar, I've had enough of this. He's going down," said Dave.

"What are you going to do?" I asked.

"This." Dave replied, swinging the giant paddle he was holding, hitting Simon on the side of his face, knocking him to the ground.

"Shit Dave! That was a bit hard," I said.

"Hard? The prick was trying to eat me!" Dave proclaimed.

Simon awkwardly rose to his feet and resumed his pursuit of Dave, the blow he took to the head, seemingly having no effect. Dave grasped the paddle with both hands and stabbed at Simon hitting him hard in the stomach. Simon arched forward and Dave swung again only this time swinging up, hitting him forcefully under the chin. The impact was such that Simon's feet left the ground flinging him backwards into the air; the back of his head cracking against the concrete as his body hit the ground. Seconds later, blood began to pour from the wound.

"Holy shit balls did you hear the sound of his head crunching against the concrete?" yelled Dave.

"This isn't good mate, there's blood pouring from the back of his head. I think he really is dead this time," I said.

Both Dave and I edged towards Simon for a closer inspection. We had not taken more than two steps when he let out a laboured groan. We both froze, reluctant to move any nearer.

"Check him then," Dave said.

"No I really think you should do it. It was you that gave him a swinging upper cut with your plastic paddle," came my reply.

Simon groaned again only this time it was accompanied with a twitch of both his arms.

43

"Exactly, I've been doing all the work, it's about time you pulled your finger out," replied Dave.

Another groan arose from Simon as he began to warily rise to his feet. Once he made it upright, he stood motionless facing Dave, giving me a clear view of the back of his sick, sweat and now blood soaked head. There was a large flap of bloodied flesh hanging from his head. Inside the wound I swear I could see his skull and what looked like a large crack running through it. Once again, I threw up, only now I had nothing left inside me. The retching noise that I made was enough to divert Simon's attention from Dave to me.

"Right, well, he looks fine to me, I think we should go," I said, with absolutely no desire to stick around any longer than I needed to.

"Come on Dave, see you tomorrow Simon, hope you feel better after the puke and shitting thing," I continued.

I turned from Simon and quickly started to walk away, back towards the alley and the graveyard of starlings. I could hear Simon's moans and the shuffling of his feet as he attempted to give chase. This was followed by a sound that I had never heard before but over the past day, I have become all too familiar with. If you combine the sounds of wading through mud with the cracking of an egg you might get pretty close. No sooner had I heard the noise, Simon's moaning came to an abrupt halt.

"Fuck me!" I heard Dave exclaim.

I turned to see what had happened to be greeted by a sight that will stay with me forever. Not because it's the most disgusting thing I've ever seen, because it isn't, not anymore. I've seen plenty of things over the past 24 hours that will make your toes curl but it was the first, and you know what they say, you never forget your first time!

Simon stood motionless, with a mayonnaise stirring paddle inserted in to the back of his head. Dave was holding on to the other end of the paddle and it was this that was keeping Simon up right. Dave lifted his right leg and placed his foot on Simon's back, pushing out with force, dislodging what remained of his head from the paddle, resulting in his falling to the floor. He wasn't getting up from this one.

"Well I wasn't expecting that to happen," Dave said, fags in hand searching his pockets for a lighter.

"Dave what have you done? You've killed him!" I panicked.

"I didn't mean too. These things are sturdier than they look," he said examining his paddle, watching as bits of Simon's face slid from the shovel headed murder weapon. *"You haven't seen my lighter have you lar? I'm dying for a bifter."*

"How can you be dying for a smoke? You've always got one hanging out of your mouth, you're never not smoking!" I said.

"Well I have just killed a man, cut me a fucking break will ya," Dave replied.

He looked to the ground and found his lighter resting in a puddle of Simon's brain juice.

"There you are," he said, bending down to retrieve it.

Dave shook the lighter in an attempt to remove the blood and chunks of head matter that clung to it but it wouldn't light. Dave threw the lighter to the ground in anger.

"Now what are we going to do?" Dave asked.

"We need to phone 999. I'll check my phone again to see if I can get a signal," I said, taking my mobile phone out of my pocket.

"Not about him dipshit about my tabs. He's dead and going nowhere, he can wait. I'm alive and in desperate need of a smoke." Dave announced.

"Look just forget about cigarettes for a minute will you?" I shouted. Dave's a great guy but Christ he can be hard work at times.

"What the fuck is going on here? First no-one comes in to work, then birds fall from the sky, then we watch Simon be violently sick …" I said.

"… And shit himself, don't forget about that," Dave interrupted.

"... Ok and shit himself. Then we watched him seemingly drown in his own puke only to recover and try to eat us, and then you killed him!" I continued.

"Hey keep it down lar, the whole world doesn't need to know," said Dave with an over the top stage whisper.

"The whole world? Look around Dave, there's no-one here. Just you, me and our dead former manager that used to have an intact head till you split it in two. What are we going to do man? We're totally fucked. I can't go to prison. Who will look after Emily? There's only my brother and he can barely look after himself let alone a teenage girl. He'd have her living in a tent and foraging up Runcorn Hill for food," I said.

"Stop panicking John we are not going to prison. It was self-defence you said it yourself Ace, the stinky shit was trying to eat us. He obviously lost his mind," Dave reasoned.

We heard a noise coming from inside the factory. It sounded like the clanging of equipment being knocked over.

"Did that come from the factory?" I asked Dave.

I knew that it did, I was just clinging to the small hope that my mind was playing tricks and I was hearing things.

"Sounded like it. I didn't see anyone else in there when I nipped in to get this paddle. Simon's always the last one

out as he has to lock up. The place should be empty Kid,"
Dave replied and we looked at each other, both of us
sharing the same look of concern.

We heard the noise again, only this time it was followed by
a loud groan similar to the noise Simon had been making.
Dave and I both looked at each other, not saying anything
but we both thought the same thing. It was happening
again. Fear had set in completely now and my hands
started to shake uncontrollably. I placed them in my
pockets before Dave could see. This situation wasn't
affecting him the same as it was me and I didn't want him
to see how distressed I had become. He had a sparkle in
his eye and a tight grip on his battle paddle, more than
ready to use it if need be. It would appear that what had
happened to Simon was not an isolated incident and it had
no doubt happened to the poor fucker lumbering his way
around the factory. The noise came again, sounding closer
this time. Whoever this was, they were heading towards
the factory door. If our recent experience had taught us
anything, it was that whoever they were, it wasn't likely
they were coming to say hello. I was half expecting them
to open the door, licking their lips, with a knife and fork in
their hands.

The groan came again, louder still and followed by a thud
that sounded like someone had fallen against the inside of
the factory door. I took a step backwards. Oh man I wish I
hadn't done that. My foot came down heavy on Simon's

neck, completely separating what remained of his head from his shoulders. I tried to steady myself but it just made things worse as my other foot came down on his skull, cracking it in two. I almost slipped as the heel of my boot trampled on what remained of his brain. You know that feeling you get when you inadvertently stand on a snail and you hear the crunch and squelch as the poor little invertebrate is ripped from life? Times that by 50! I gagged so hard I thought my stomach was going to spill out of my mouth. Dave turned to see why I was making such a commotion only to find that I was bent over, retching my guts up with tears in my eyes, partly from the strain and partly from the situation.

Dave looked me up and down. *"Nice shoes,"* he said, before turning his attention back to the factory door. I looked down to see that my boots were lodged inside the two separated halves of Simon's head, making it look like I was wearing a pair of novelty slippers. I imagined my toes squishing around the insides of Simon's face and I completely freaked, kicking out as hard as I could in an attempt to dislodge my boots. My left boot came out no problem, sending one half of Simon's head skidding across the car park, but my right boot? Not so much. I shook my right foot wildly, a frenzy taking over. My body jerking like someone had simultaneously poured cold water down my back and placed a rat inside my jeans. If this was New York City in the early 1980s, I'd be king of the breakdancing scene with the moves I was popping. But it wasn't. It was

2013 and I was wiggling about uncontrollably trying to remove my boot from the inside of a man's head. I kicked out with so much force that Simon's face flew from my boot, whizzing past Dave's head then hitting the factory door before resting on the ground.

"Hey! Careful kidda, you nearly hit me then. Watch where you're kicking next time," said Dave, breaking his fixation on the factory door or more importantly, what was behind it.

"Next time? Christ Dave I'm hoping there won't be a next time. Look, let's just get out of here ok? As I soon as I get a phone signal I'll call the police and explain everything that's happened," I said.

"Don't you want to see who's behind the door?" Dave asked, an inquisitive glint in his eye.

"All I care about right now is getting home to my daughter and changing these boots. It's starting to feel like juice from Simon's head is seeping through my socks to my toes. So no Dave, in answer to your question, I have absolutely no desire what-so-ever to find out who is behind that door," I said, turning my back on Dave and the horror scene that lay before me.

I began to walk away, again heading towards the alley and starling graveyard, when I heard the loud thud of something large banging against the factory door and it swinging open.

"Well fuck me look who it is," came Dave's response.

I didn't want to look. Why would I? It obviously wasn't going to be a welcoming sight now was it? I stood for a second, eyes closed, just listening to the moans behind me. I gulped and slowly turned to see what fresh kind of hell lay in waiting.

Slouched in the now open factory doorway was the intimidating bulk of Paul Brockway, one of the factory engineers. If any of the packing lines were having problems with machinery, Paul was your guy, but you had to find him first. The fact that he was so elusive was probably why neither Dave nor I had realised he had made it into work that day. This guy was like the Scarlet Pimpernel and as elusive as a ninja, which is quite the achievement given his mammoth size. Paul, or 'Brockers' as he is more commonly known, is at least 6ft 7inches and is as wide as he is tall. Not an ounce of fat on him either. Quite astonishing really as he would be the first to tell you *(when you could find him)* that he didn't exercise - instead he concentrated all of his efforts into getting through the day expelling as little energy as possible. Not doing anything and getting away with it is something Brockers was extremely proud of and he wore his laziness like a badge of honour.

This guy had work licked. The packing lines within the factory are old and constantly breaking down but the failure of machinery was never anything serious and was usually something that could be repaired quite quickly. Because the staff on the packing lines had got so used to Brockers never being around, they would always fix the problem themselves, not even attempting to find him. Why bother spending the best part of your shift searching for the invisible man when you can have the problem fixed yourself within minutes? This was a win/win situation for him. The packing lines kept running and management were none the wiser. How did he get away with it? Intimidation. The guy was a man mountain and staff wouldn't dare report him to management.

The only time anyone would ever see him would be during lunch time when he would barge through the canteen doors, sit at whichever was the busiest table, TAKE someone's newspaper then draw dicks on the heads of the people in every picture. It didn't matter who they were as he didn't discriminate. Picture of the Queen – Dick on the head. Picture of the Pope – Dick on the head. The Dalai Lama – Dick on the head. If the picture had a head, then that head was getting a dick, but not just any old crappy cartoon child drawing of a dick. These bad boys were a work of art. Shading, texture, veins... If he put as much effort into his work as he did his fascination with drawing dicks he could have been a great engineer. But that's the thing with Brockers, he just loved the lash too much.

As I turned to look at him, the first thing I noticed was his complexion, as it was almost identical to Simon's. His eyes were white in colour and sunken in appearance and his skin tone was again almost translucent giving a clear view of the veins beneath his flesh. Unfortunately, I could no longer use Simon's head to compare the two as one half was somewhere across the car park and the other, although resting at the feet of Brockers, was so badly mashed it looked like a bag of chopped liver.

The big man started to sniff the air, moving his head from side to side with gloops of saliva dripping from his mouth. He let out a harrowing groan then bent his upper body forward closer to the ground. Something had alerted his nostrils. Dave and I watched silently as Brockers slowly got down on his knees and scooped up the remains of Simon's head, sniffing it extensively. I honestly thought he was going to eat it, but instead he threw it to the ground, showing absolutely no interest in chowing down on Simon's putrid face.

I tried to speak but nothing would come.

"Dave," I mouthed, but no sound followed. A crippling panic had possessed me, crushing my ability to communicate.

Come on John get a grip and man up I thought to myself.

A stern self-talking to now given, I took a breath and swallowed, preparing myself to try again.

"Dave," I squeaked, this time making the smallest of noises.

Dave completely ignored me, obviously mistaking my new found manly voice for that of a mouse or squirrel. Brockers heard me though, and he let out a loud groan, spit dripping from his mouth as he looked right at me.

"Dave!" I yelped, slightly more pleased with the tone of this one, my pitch changing from that of a two year old to a pubescent teenager.

Brockers opened his mouth wide, letting out an almighty roar. Similar to Simon, he shuffled forward with little co-ordination but none the less he was heading my way and after turning down Simon's head as his starter, he had clearly chosen me for his main. Not surprisingly, I was once again frozen to the spot.

"Dave!" I croaked.

"Dave!" finally, making a sound audible enough to grab his attention, he snapped out of his fixation with Brockers, looked over to me and noticed how petrified I was.

"Oi Brockers!" Dave shouted, *"You should always look at the menu before deciding on your meal lar. There's more of me than him."*

Brockers took the bait, changed course and began shuffling his size sixteen's towards Dave. After eyeing up both of his options, the big guy obviously decided that

Dump Truck was the tastier meal option. Dave, battle paddle in hand, was gearing himself up for a fight and was quite prepared to stand his ground against this monster of a man.

Watching Dave being so fearless suddenly snapped me out of my panic induced statuesque statue. Dave had just put himself in harm's way to save me and I was damned if I wasn't going to return the favour. I looked around for something, anything that resembled a weapon. There was nothing. I contemplated trying to rip off one of Simon's arms but who was I kidding. Jam jar lids get the better of me on a daily basis *(so I eat a lot jam, got a problem with that? Well I would eat a lot if could I get the damn lids off!)*, there was little chance that I could pull a dead man's arm out of its socket. Then I saw it! I turned and ran towards Simon's car as fast as I could whilst being careful not to slip in the puddle of puke and shit in front of it. I grabbed the dead starling that had landed on the roof of thr car and ran back to my previous position

"I'll save you buddy!" I shouted and then I threw the dead bird at Brockers, hitting him on the back of the head.

Brockers stopped walking towards Dave, turned around and restarted his pursuit of me.

"Oh Shit!" I said, realising that my attempts at being heroic were not only rather pathetic but have now put me right back on the dead man's menu.

I looked around again, frantically trying to find something I could throw or hit him with. To my left, on the far side of the car park was the other part of Simon's head that I had kicked away earlier. Was it not enough to dismember the poor fella, wear his head as slippers, kick one half across the car park and the other at the factory door? No? I didn't think so either, so I ran to where the head lay and grabbed it by its hair as it was the only part I could even consider touching. I knelt down and positioned it on the ground as close to standing upright as possible. Dave watched on, a smile on his face, loving every minute of what he was seeing.

I took five steps backward, licked my finger and placed it in the air to check for wind direction. This was more for Dave's benefit than anything else. I could see he was enjoying this and he knew exactly what I was going to do.

"Cop a load of this you big bastard!" I shouted as I ran forward, booting Simon's head as hard I could in the direction of Brockers.

Both Dave and I watched as Simon's head flew through the air, bits of blood and lumps of face flying off in every direction. I can't talk for Dave but the head seemed to glide through the air in slow motion as it made its way towards the intended target. Brockers continued to lurch forward unaware of the fleshy missile heading his way.

I couldn't have asked for a better hit and I would never be able to make that shot again in a million years. Simon's manky, blood dripping half head came down from the sky and hit Brockers square in the face knocking him on his backside. He sat there for a second as if stunned and disorientated by what just happened.

"Go ed lad!" shouted Dave, waving his paddle in the air with approval.

The big man again began to sniff the air, following his nose and reaching out with his hands until they found the remaining half of Simon's cursed head. Just like before, Brockers sniffed at it, then turned his nose up, throwing the head to the ground. Picky bastard!

"Lost your appetite big man?" shouted Dave.

Brockers immediately turned his head and gazed in my friend's direction. It was at that point I started to think that something must be wrong with his eyesight. During his transition from a lazy penis-drawing obsessed engineer to that of a disgusting looking, sunken eyed, pale skinned devil beast *(probably still with a love of the lash)*, something had effected his ability to see, making him more reliant on sound and smells than sight. But how bad was his eyesight? Could he see at all or had his vision gone completely? I didn't want to get close enough to find out.

Brockers started to move in an attempt to rise to his feet. The big man fell to his left side then rolled over on to his front, then rolled onto his back again. He then attempted to sit up but he was just too big and lacked the co-ordination to do it. Both Dave and I could see what he was trying and failing to do. We both approached, making sure we were more than a grabbing distance away.

"Do you think he's trying to get up?" I offered.

"Looks like it kidda. Are you not going to help him?" Dave responded.

"I'll pass thanks Dave, I don't fancy having my arm chewed off for my efforts. Have you seen the colour of his eyes? They're covered with a milky glaze. Do you think he can see properly? He looks to be following his nose more than anything," I said.

"Let's find out then shall we?" said Dave as he closed in on Brockers.

"I don't think that's a good idea Dave." I said as he began motioning to me with his hand to be quiet and offering a look that said he knows what he's doing. I wasn't so sure!

Dave moved within touching distance of Brockers, who appeared to be more concerned with getting back on his feet than the potential meal that was now right in front of him. Dave turned his head towards me and smiled. For a moment I thought I was right, the big guy's vision wasn't what it was. Maybe he couldn't see at all. But then, in a flash, everything changed.

Brockers, with speed, reached out and grabbed Dave's leg, pulling him to the ground. Before I could process what was happening, Brockers pulled Dave towards him and bit down hard on his boot.

"I thought you said he couldn't see?" Dave yelled.

"I didn't think he could, I'm as surprised as you are!" I replied.

"I fucking doubt that lar," came the reply.

Brockers was chewing on Dave's boot like a dog with a bone, spittle and drool pouring from his mouth. With his free leg, Dave repeatedly kicked out, smashing Brockers in the head over and over again. Every kick inflicting more and more damage to the big guy's already disgusting face but it made little difference. There was no way on this cursed earth that he was letting go of Dave's boot without a fight.

Dave had dropped his paddle during the struggle and it had fallen out of his reach but not mine. I grabbed the paddle and thrust it as hard as I could into the mouth of the behemoth, freeing Dave's boot as a consequence. The force in which I rammed the paddle into the big guy's mouth shattered his teeth completely. No-one told Brockers this though as he lay on his back, squirming and chomping on the paddle which I now had firmly lodged in his orifice. I stood over him, paddle held vertically with the shovel end wedged between his jaws. I placed my foot on the ridge of the paddle, closed my eyes and using it as a spade, pushed down as hard as I could, forcing it through his mouth and the back of his head. Thank god I had my eyes closed. The crunch and scraping sound that accompanied my actions sent shivers down my spine. I opened my eyes to bear witness to my actions. My former work mate, well colleague as he didn't actually do any work, lay dead with his head from the jaw up separated from the rest of his body.

"Well he was a hungry hippo wasn't he?" Dave said, again assessing the damage as only he could.

Then suddenly it came to me, fear subsided sufficiently enough for my mind to process cognitive thought. Did I know what was happening? Could it be the thing my brother and I had talked about all these years? Let's look at what was happening here. Nobody came into work, I've watched a man apparently die only to rise up and try to eat Dave *(that should have been the first fucking sign to be honest, but when you're actually in this kind of situation, your brain doesn't operate as it should)* and the only way we stopped him was by smashing a blunt instrument through his skull. Then the whole thing happened again! It had to be. My mind raced trying to find another, more rational explanation for what was happening but nothing came. Fuck! If I was right then Brockers had Dave's foot in his mouth. Had he been bitten? Was he infected? Is that how this thing even worked? I had to find out.

"Dave are you ok, have you been bitten?" I frantically asked, looking him over for any signs of bite or scratch marks.

"Eh? No Ace I'm fine. Steel toe caps these lar," he said showing me his boots, *"The greedy shit hardly made a dent."*

"What about your legs? He was grabbing at you wasn't he? Have you been scratched?" I asked.

"John I'm fine, don't worry. I'm not infected." Dave replied as if discussing the price of milk.

"That's good. Eh? You know?" I replied, both shocked and confused that Dave might have already worked out what was happening.

"Know what? That Simon and Brockers were zombies? Of course I know. What else do you think's going on here?" Dave said, whilst bending down searching through the trouser and jacket pockets of Brockers.

"Well wha.. whe... how... how long have you known?" I asked.

Not the greatest sentence I've ever constructed but my mind was doing loops trying to come to terms with the fact that Dave had figured all this out before me and he didn't seem remotely fazed by any of it.

"I don't know lar, I probably realised when Simon tried to eat me. It's a classic case," Dave replied.

"Classic case? You make it sound like we have zombie outbreaks every other day!" I said.

"We've all seen zombie films. Hollywood has been preparing us for this shit for years. Dawn of the Dead, Day of the dead, Diary of the Dead, Zombieland, 28 Days Later, the list goes on kidda. The fucking Walking Dead is on the TV every week and you're wondering how I managed to figure this out?' Dave explained.

He had a point. Maybe all the zombie movies, TV shows, books, comics and graphic novels that we all love so dearly, have just been propaganda to slowly condition us into being prepared for the coming apocalypse.

"Are you gonna help me or what?" said Dave, becoming slightly agitated.

"What are you looking for?" I replied.

"A lighter, I'm sure Brockers smoked."

The man is a machine!

I bent down and helped Dave search Zombie Brockers for a lighter.

"Were you planning on telling me you'd figured all this out or did you think you'd wait until I was having my brains *munched on first?"* I asked, pulling out a picture of an expertly drawn penis from one of Brockers' pockets.

"I knew you'd get there eventually. I was having too much fun watching the confusion on your face," replied Dave, finding a packet of cigarettes but no lighter. *"Not my brand but I'll take what I can get."*

"This is serious Dave. Fucking zombies mate." Panic returning, images of my daughter trapped running through my mind.

"I know," Dave casually replied, pulling out car keys from Brockers jacket pocket. *"What kind of arse smokes and doesn't carry a lighter on him?"*

"We've got to get out of here. I've got to get to Emily," I said, rising back to my feet.

"I'm with you lar. We're not walking though; we have no idea how bad this situation really is. I've got the big guys car keys here," said Dave with a smile as he looked over to the factory car park.

There were two cars in the car park. One car was a luxury four wheel drive Range Rover, perfect for on and off road driving with five star comforts and it belonged to Brockers. The other was Simon's Ford Thunderbird, perfect if it was 1983 and you were not a fan of suspension or safety. I can't drive, never had so much as a lesson. Dave can though, so I felt the decision on which car to take should fall firmly on his shoulders.

Dave and I walked over to the car park and eyed up both options. Dave smiled at me, then pressed the key fob on the keys he had taken from Brockers. The Range Rover's doors unlocked and Dave walked over to the vehicle, opened the driver's door and climbed inside.

"Thank god," I said, *"I thought you were going to choose the Thunderbird for a second."*

Dave then stepped out of the Range Rover holding a lighter in his hand.

"I am choosing the Thunderbird! I knew he'd have a lighter somewhere," he said lighting a cigarette, taking in a long pull of nicotine. *"What? You didn't honestly think we'd be leaving in that monstrosity did you?"*

"Well, yes I did actually if I'm honest with you," I replied.

"No chance Ace, we wouldn't make it out of the car park in that thing," Dave replied, booting the Range Rover.

"Why what's wrong with it?" I asked.

"Well it hasn't got a cassette player for one," he replied.

I thought about arguing with him but really what was the point? The Thunderbird was an 80s classic; of course Dave was going to opt for it over the luxury, executive, comfy, and perfect for our potentially hazardous journey Range Rover. The Thunderbird could have been up against a Bugatti Veyron and still won.

Dave walked over to Simon's Thunderbird and retrieved the keys from the puddle of puke. He then walked back over to Brockers and wiped the keys on the dead man's jacket, removing any dripping gloop. Dave took a moment to look over our former colleague, noticing a permanent marker in the big guy's shirt pocket. He took the pen, removed the lid and drew a massive penis on the amputated forehead of Brockers.

"It's what he would have wanted. Come on Ace let's go!" he said, throwing to the floor what little remained of his cigarette and marching over to the Thunderbird.

I took one last look at the massacre of human and feathered corpses that filled my vision. Everywhere I looked, I could see death. Directly in front of me was Simon, beyond him was Brockers and littered all over the car park were dead starlings. For the first time, I had a chance to take stock. This was real. This was really happening. Zombies. FUCKING ZOMBIES! My brother had talked about this day since we were children and as unbelievable as all this seemed, it had happened and it was here. The crazy bastard was right! I had to find my daughter and then get to my brother's house.

Dave opened one of the back passenger doors and slid his battle paddle inside. It had already proved to be a formidable weapon and one that we would no doubt need again, even if it did look like a giant's teaspoon.

He sat in the driver's seat, closed the car door and fastened his seat belt. For only the second time today, Dave removed his sunglasses, turning to face me. He meant business.

"Listen lar, what we've just been through, well nobody should have to experience that. It was fucking awful to say the least. The way Simon's skull split in two when I rammed the paddle straight through the back of his head, and the sound when it cracked open, oh man that was grim. Then there's what you did to Brockers...' the look on my face must have said it all as Dave stopped in his tracks, probably sensing that I might throw up again.

I really didn't need a reminder of how we had just brutally murdered two work colleagues. Ok, they *were* technically zombies and one of them was a complete prick but still, I'd never so much as killed a spider before *(Emily does that for me but keep that to yourself ok?)*. Thinking about what I'd done gave me a numbness like I had never experienced before. Did I feel any guilt for my actions? Not at all. Brockers would have killed Dave. The big man had to die, again! The same can be said for Simon but as I only removed his head from his neck then wore its two halves as slippers, you'll have to ask 80s Dave as to how he feels about killing him. But he looked like he enjoyed it.

"Look Ace, what I'm trying to say is that all this that we've just been through, everything we've had to do, it's probably only the tip of the iceberg and if this thing's as bad as I'm expecting it to be well, I want to make sure you're ready.' Dave said, sensing that maybe I needed preparing for Armageddon and he was right.

Of course I did, who wouldn't? A normal day for me would be to get out of bed, try to wake Emily up, fail, try again, fail again then bang repeatedly on her bedroom door until she finally woke from her slumber. Then I'd make us breakfast, see her off to school and go to work where I would eat disgusting mayonnaise all day before going home to cook a meal for us both. Then watch TV for a few hours and finally, go to bed. Place that day on repeat and you had my life. Captain uneventful that was me, busy sailing along on the good ship average. I thought myself normal, just like everyone else and I liked it. I was happy with my life. Sure it was tough at times being a single parent but things were about to get a hell of a lot tougher, and I needed to be prepared.

"I'm anything but ready if I'm honest with you Dave. I mean, Christ man, zombies! I've been listening to my brother talk about this day all my life but I never thought it would ever happen. It's one of those impossible scenarios that you hear people talk about to pass the time. Just like

discussing what you would do if you won the lottery or if you found out you had a long lost rich relative that died and left you their fortune. You know, the kind of stuff that would never happen but you talk about how awesome it would be if it did. Well as it turns out zombies, are not awesome." I replied.

"They are a little bit," Dave offered, a smile on his face obviously trying to lighten the mood.

"I don't know what your plans are Dave but I need to get to my Daughter. I need to make sure she's ok," I said.

"No worries Kidda. Don't you worry about your daughter, we'll find her," Dave reassured me.

He placed his sunglasses back over his eyes and revved the engine of the Ford Thunderbird. The whole car began to shake so badly I thought it was about to fall apart. Then the exhausted backfired.

"Listen to that engine purr. Fucking marvellous!" Dave shouted.

I felt safer outside than I did in this death trap. I needed to find Emily and I was having serious doubts that this old banger would make it ten yards, never mind all the way to her school.

"I've always wanted to drive Simon's car. Out of all the things that I hated about him, by far my biggest grudge

bear was the fact he owned this car and I didn't. Ah well, it's mine now lar," he said triumphantly.

"Dave, do you not want to check on your family?" I shouted over the noise of the car engine.

"Family? You mean my olds? Fuck them lar. They don't give a shit about me, never have. Why should I care what happens to them? They're in Liverpool anyway; I could never get there in time. No mate, let's go and get Emily, she'll be needing her dad," Dave replied.

He didn't want to discuss his family and I wasn't going to push him further on the topic. He opened the glove compartment of the Thunderbird.

"Let's see what music old blister face liked to listen to shall we," he said, pulling out a selection of cassette tapes and vetting them intently.

"The greatest hits of Curtis Steiger, Always and Forever: Best love songs of all time, Titanic: The motion Picture soundtrack… it just goes on. There's even a Cliff Richard album in here. Well now I feel even less sorry that he turned into a zombie and I had to kill him," Dave said as he unzipped his bum bag and took out a cassette tape, placing it into the tape player, his finger hovering over the play button.

"Before I press play on the greatest song ever written in the history of everything, where are we going Ace?" He asked

"The Grange. Emily went back to school today after half term so she'll be there, hopefully," I answered.

"No worries kidda, now strap yourself in because this song is going to blow your cock off!" Dave proclaimed.

Dave pressed play on the cassette player and 'Are Friends Electric' by Gary Numan came screaming out of the car stereo. Considering how old the stereo was it handled Dave turning the volume up to eleven quite well. Dave put his foot down and the Thunderbird jolted into action as we sped out of the factory car park.

It was time to find Emily.

Read all about it

It was early Monday morning and for many, the start of a new working week. Not for Barry Owens. Monday morning was the same as every morning for Barry as his routine hadn't changed for over thirty years.

Barry had opened BJ & J Owens, a small newsagent on Balfour Street, in 1981 and from 06:00am to 07:00pm every day since, he had been serving the local community. Baz's, as the shop was known locally, was an institution in the town of Runcorn. Whatever you couldn't get from the bigger shops, he would sell. Suitcase tags, cotton, string, envelopes of every size, children's books, chalk, Space Raider crisps, geometry sets, single toilet rolls... he sold everything. Oh, and you could also buy a newspaper and a pint of milk. This meant that his customers would vary greatly. It wouldn't be uncommon to see a queue in Baz's consisting of pensioners buying a newspaper, children wanting sweets, builders purchasing an 'adult' magazine and workers paying for a pint of milk and a pot noodle. Also on Balfour Street was a Co-operative supermarket and it was a testament to him that customers would snub the larger 'chain' supermarket to shop at his smaller independent newsagent.

It was now 06:35am and he was behind the counter sorting out the morning papers for delivery before his paperboy, Josh arrived. Music would normally be the morning accompaniment for Barry and his radio would usually be playing classic rock 'n' roll. It reminded him of his younger years in the 1960's when he played guitar in his band 'The BJ's' long before his responsibilities as a parent and business owner.

He switched on the old battered medium wave radio but it only broadcast white noise. No matter which station he tried to tune in, the result was the same and he assumed that his trusted radio had finally had its day. He mused to himself that today was going to be a bad day and his radio would only be the start of things going wrong. How right he was.

It was a part of his job that he had done so many times before that he went through the motions automatically, sorting and numbering newspapers to be delivered without having to refer to his order book. He knew the name and address of everyone in his book; he could even tell you which newspapers they had delivered. He had gone so far into autopilot that he hadn't noticed the headlines on every paper told the same story.

'Russian virus spreads throughout Europe' – The Daily Mail

'Human Super Plague arrives!' – The Mirror

'Death toll rises as disease spreads – The Times

'Posh Spice in sex video shocker' – The Daily Sport

Barry, like the majority of the UK had watched, read and listened to reports of a new 'Super Plague' that had been spreading throughout Europe and like most, had not taken any of it seriously. Mad cow disease had been and gone, bird flu was in and out of the news more than Katie Price's breasts, there were new strains of hospital superbugs being announced on what seemed like a weekly basis, but Barry was still here. As far as he and a great deal of the UK were concerned, it was just scare mongering on behalf of the news corporations and he wasn't about to stay at home and hide away under a blanket until the television told him it was safe again. He had a business to run.

He was organising the newspaper deliveries for Oxford Road when he heard the shop door open and he glanced to see who it was. A small hooded figure stumbled through the door and stalled by the ice cream freezer in the middle of the shop floor.

"I'll have these ready for you in a second Josh," he said without looking at the boy.

Josh Brown had worked for Barry since he was fourteen years of age. Now aged sixteen, his paperboy days were coming to an end but he had been a good worker for Barry, having never missed a shift and, unlike some of his other paperboys, he never dumped the morning deliveries onto the railway tracks behind the shop just so he could go back to bed for an hour before school.

"You're a bit early Josh. Was it the excitement of delivering the morning papers that got you out of bed or was it

something else?" Barry asked, again continuing to sort the newspapers without visually acknowledging the boy.

"Gurumphrrhh."

Barry had never heard a noise like that before and it was enough to distract him from his duties and for the first time look properly at Josh. He couldn't see the boy's face. The hood from his jacket and his slouched posture had aided in shadowing his features sufficiently. He watched as Josh stood, unsteadily by the ice cream freezer, gurgling growls projecting from his mouth.

"Are you ok Josh?"

He could sense that there was something not right with the boy but there was nothing that could have prepared him for what happened next.

Josh lunged forward, hands reaching out towards Barry, his face still covered by his hood. The only thing between him and his employer was the shop counter, and Barry would soon be thankful that the hatch was lowered and Josh could not reach him.

Barry reached for the screwdriver he kept next to the till and with it, carefully removed the hood from Josh's face. What he saw sent shivers down his spine. Josh was gnarling and chattering his teeth together frantically; dried blood coating his mouth and chin. Barry noted that it was unlikely that the blood belonged to Josh as he had no cuts or injuries that were visible. So what did that mean? Had he been fighting? He didn't think so. The way Josh was intent on grabbing him and the manner in which he was chomping his gnashers presented only one conclusion. He had bitten someone, or worse eaten someone, and now Barry was the next meal on his menu.

Barry reached for the broom he kept behind the counter and with it, pushed out at Josh, sending him falling backwards into the ice cream freezer. Josh lifted himself up and staggered back towards Barry retaking his previous position. Barry pushed out with the broom again, this time putting all of his strength behind the shove. Josh stumbled backwards and he fell, cracking the back of his head on the shop shelving.

He winced when he heard the crunching sound of the boy's skull cracking against the metal unit. Blood began to pour from Josh's head spilling out on to the shop floor. Barry immediately felt regret, not because he had causing what could be a fatal injury, but because his floor was now covered in blood and it would be a bugger to clean.

Barry moved to check on his paperboy and hopefully stop any more blood from ruining the floor. His actions were halted as Josh began to move, his head making a 'slurping' sound as it lifted out of the growing puddle of sticky blood.

Barry was having difficulty in believing what he was witnessing. The injury Josh had sustained should have been enough to keep him down but here he was, back on his feet and once again, coming at him. He moved behind the counter and closed the hatch; securing himself from the paperboy. Josh stumbled forward, banging into the counter with arms reaching out, hands clawing the air in front of his employer. Barry picked up the telephone to call the police for help but there was no dial tone.

"Oh bollocks!" he said, realising he was on his own with this.

He looked down at the newspapers on the counter and for the first time, properly registered the printed headlines. He then repeated his last four actions again and again.

Josh

Telephone

Radio

Papers

Josh

Telephone

Radio

Papers ...

The clogs in his mind slowly began to turn and place everything together, then the door to the shop opened slightly and through the small gap a skin torn, blood stained hand attached to a shredded arm appeared, slowly followed by the gaunt dead face of man he knew very well. It was Paul Smith, one of his regular customers and an old friend. He noted the wound on Paul's hand and furthermore, his arm, resembled deep cuts made by scratching. He moved his attention back to Josh who was still grasping at the air in front of his face. There was dried blood on Josh's hands and, more importantly, what resembled human flesh under his fingernails.

"Did you do this to Paul?" he asked the non-responsive Josh.

Paul lurched forwarded, joining Josh up against the counter, grabbing at Barry who was for now safe with the hatch down. Barry had always been a man who trusted his instinct and gone with his gut and his gut was telling him that something quite horrible had happened to his paperboy and friend. He was starting to think that the two people who stood before him were not the people he knew and that Josh and Paul, were no more. He didn't yet know what had happened to them but he knew he had to do something before it happened to him.

"Sorry Josh," he said apologising for what he was about to do.

He grabbed the screwdriver and stabbed Josh through his right eye and into the kid's brain, killing him instantly. He watched, filled with remorse as Josh fell backwards, hitting the floor behind him, a screwdriver protruding from his right eye socket. Barry didn't have time for wallowing in regret. Not yet at least as he now had Paul to deal with.

Since opening the shop in 1981, Barry had dealt with many an idiot. Just in case things should ever become violent, he kept a weapon underneath the counter, always within arm's reach but he had never used it. Now it was finally going to see some action.

He reached under the shop counter and retrieved an axe handle.

"Sorry old friend," he said and with both hands gripping the axe handle, he brought it crashing down on Paul's head, shattering his skull on impact.

Before he could process what had happened, the shop door opened again and this time, in staggered another of his locals, Jenna Zannin–Jones, munching on a dismembered tattooed hand.

"Christ not you too!" he sighed, not only referring to Jenna, but to the hand she had hanging from her mouth.

He recognised the heavily tattooed hand as belonging to Neil Murphy, an eccentric local that would frequent the shop early mornings to buy cigarettes after returning from working his 'cabaret' act. By day, Neil was a vegan metal head who kept himself to himself. By night he was Belinda

Blaze, the fire haired drag queen of Manchester's gay district.

On seeing the hand and knowing Neil as well as he did, he mused that should his transvestite customer have survived the attack, he would be more concerned on how he would look in his many spectacular outfits than losing a limb.

Jenna slowly staggered forward; Neil's tattooed yet beautifully manicured hand flapping in her mouth. She had little concern for her surroundings. So much so that she bumbled closer, mouth full of hand and arms outstretched, reaching for Barry. Ignorant to the dead bodies that lay in her path, her left foot came down hard on the mashed head of Paul and she fell down rolling around uncontrollably, unable to get to her feet.

"I'm sorry Jenna," Barry said, regretful for what he had to do.

He tightened his grip on the gore stained axe handle then repeatedly smashed her over the head until she was once again, dead. Barry assessed the damage he had created, surmising that he had probably gone into overkill and hit Jenna several more times than was necessary. He could tell this by the blancmange that used to be her head.

"That's going to need bleaching," he said to himself, evaluating the blood and brain matter that covered the floor.

It was then he heard a heavy *'thud'* that sounded like something large hitting the outside of the shop. He climbed over the heap of dead customers and opened the shop door, stepping outside on to investigate.

A car had ploughed into the house next to his shop. Behind the wheel, strapped into the driver's seat, head resting on an inflated airbag was another regular customer of BJ & J Owens, Courtney Dunbavand. The zombie that was formally Courtney's boyfriend, Chris Jackson, was in the front passenger seat. Having ripped open her stomach, he was pouring handfuls of her intestines into his putrid mouth.

Barry approached the car and opened the front passenger door, dragging Chris out from the vehicle and onto the path. With his trusted axe handle, he brought it down on Chris's face again and again, blood and brains spraying out, coating his trousers. Eyes wide and panting heavily from exertion, he looked upon the pulped mush that was once Chris's face and adrenaline filling his tired body.

"Who's fucking next?" he yelled, waving the axe handle in the air.

Courtney's head lifted from the inflated airbag and small rasping groans left her throat. Barry heard the noise and turned to see her pale, translucent face and sunken white eyes glaring back at him. He moved to the driver's door and smashed the window with his axe handle. The newly undead Courtney turned her head to face him whilst frantically trying to wriggle free from the belt securing her to the seat. Upon smashing the car window, shards of glass tore into her face, making her once soft and blemish free skin resemble a badly assembled glass mosaic.

Tightening the grip on his weapon he forcefully jabbed it into Courtney's face repeatedly until she was no more.

Stepping away from the vehicle, he looked up and down Balfour Street, several of the infected were wandering the street. He could hear the faint cries of people shouting for help and the screams of those being eaten alive.

"When hell is full, the dead will walk the Earth," he said to himself, repeating a saying he had heard somewhere many years ago but could not recall where.

"Well not in my shop they won't!" he said, defiantly.

Barry returned to his newsagents and one by one, dragged the dead bodies of Josh, Paul and Jenna through the door, dumping them on the street outside. He entered the shop again then re-emerged holding a can of black spray paint. With it he wrote on the front of his shop...

'NO ZOMBIES!'

... then Barry returned to his newsagents, shutting the door behind him.

Journal entry 3

Dave drove the Ford Thunderbird out of the factory car park, leaving the zombie bloodbath behind us, the sounds of Gary Numan crackling from the ancient car stereo. There are two roads that run through Astmoor industrial estate. There's the main road that is roughly a mile long and goes straight through the heart of the industrial estate, giving access to all the major factories situated there. The other road is for buses only and runs adjacent to the main road but cuts through housing estates at either end of Astmoor, giving direct access to Runcorn town centre. We decided on using the bus lane, not only because it's the quickest route but also because we thought there would less chance of bumping into any dead folk that might be looking for a spot of lunch! Luckily for us, we were right and the bus lane was clear as long as you discount the many dead birds that littered the road. Not just starlings this time either. There were pigeons and crows also. Their feathered bodies tested the Thunderbird's already questionable suspension as we drove over them. Every time the wheels hit a bird, my stomach would churn, sending a cold shiver down my back. Why was it that I had quickly gotten over brutally killing Brockers but driving over dead animals was sending me to pukesville? Dave on the other hand, wasn't fazed in the slightest. Sunglasses on and fag in mouth, Dave was quite happy driving along, nodding his head in time to the synth-tastic sounds of 'Are Friends Electric'. What had happened to these birds? Had whatever had caused the zombie outbreak also affected animals? It appeared that way and if so, will they too come back from the dead? Not from what we had seen but then again, the only animals we had encountered were that of the small feathered variety.

We reached the end of the industrial estate, arriving at traffic lights that sat in front of a cross roads. Turning right would take us directly into Runcorn town centre. Turning left would take us to the many housing estates that make up the town. Directly ahead was the continuing bus lane. We needed to go left as this was the only route to Emily's school. Only advancing in any direction was going to prove difficult as directly in front of us in the crossroads, a bus lay turned on its side. Blood soaked shattered glass glistened in the winter sunlight as it littered the road. Dave turned off the cassette player as we observed the wreckage.

"What do you think happened?" I asked.

"Well if I had to hazard a guess, I'd say it crashed," Dave said, obviously trying to get a rise out of me.

"Really Dave? I thought the bus had just got tired and decided to lie down and have a little rest. The crash, what do you think caused the crash?" I said.

"Alright narky arse, calm down. I'm only trying to put a smile on that face of yours. You look like you've just had a

rectal examination and the doctor left his finger in a few minutes longer than he should have," Dave replied.

I didn't answer. How he was managing to find humour in what quite possibly is the end of the world I don't know but I appreciated what he was trying to do. Yes I was stressed and extremely scared. Not knowing if you'll ever see your daughter again is a frightful experience and one that I would never wish on anyone. That said, if you've survived long enough to be reading this journal then it's almost guaranteed you've lost someone along the way.

"What do you reckon lar? I could drive around it?" he said.

He was right, there was sufficient room for him to drive around the wreckage. What worried me was what lay on the other side. From our position all we could see was the bus and what looked like the hunched bodies of people inside. But were they dead? Alive? Dead and alive? We simply didn't know. I nodded to Dave, suggesting that he proceed with the route as planned and drive around the wreckage.

Dave edged the Ford Thunderbird forward slowly, the sheer horror of the crash becoming more apparent the closer we got. The bus had fallen on its right side after hitting the partition railings in the centre of the bus lane before skidding into the cross roads. Inside the bus towards the rear, kids were piled on top of each other and they were dead. It was horrible. Their bodies tangled with each other making it difficult to tell where one ended and another began. What I did notice was the school uniforms. These kids went to the Grange, the same school as my daughter. These kids could be my daughter's friends, Emily's class mates. Shit I might have known some of them! My heart sank thinking about it. It also meant that if these kids had taken the bus to school, then this accident happened hours ago as it was now lunchtime. I watched intently as the Thunderbird slowly moved past the rear of the upturned bus. The kid's features were hard to determine through the shattered glass and blood sodden faces but I could count at least six that had been killed in the smash. Something about the crash wasn't making sense. Yes the bus had crashed through the railings and landed on its side but that didn't seem enough to kill these kids. Their injuries appeared too severe for the accident. As we moved forward, the rest of the bus appeared empty with no other passengers visible.

"Any movement Ace?" Dave asked, concentrating on his driving.

"No movement," I replied.

If Dave had not seen the horror inside the bus I wasn't about to alert him to it. What good would seeing something like that do? The car moved at a snail's pace as we drove along the side of the bus, the road beyond the accident becoming more visible with every movement. Then Dave brought the vehicle to halt.

"What is ..." my question was muted as Dave placed his hand across my mouth.

With his spare hand he pointed forward, all the while not taking his eyes from the road ahead. I looked to see a pair of blue trouser covered legs where visible lying on the road in front of the bus. The rest of the body was obscured from our view by the vehicle. From what we could see one of the legs appeared to be twitching, almost like something or someone was tugging on it. Dave carefully opened his car door, trying to be as quiet as possible. Not easy when the door you are opening belongs to a 1983 Ford Thunderbird but I'll give Dave credit, he managed to keep the groans and croaks of the rusty door to a minimum. Me? I didn't have the same skill as when I opened my door, it sounded like a cat being skinned alive. Dave gave me a look that said if he was close enough, he would have given me a slap and who could blame him, I would have slapped me too.

We cautiously walked forward, the body in the road becoming more visible with every step. First we saw the legs, then the waist, then the arms that were tearing into the dead man's stomach, then the face of the school girl who was shovelling intestines and guts into her mouth like she was devouring sausage links.

"Someone's hungry," Dave whispered.

"It's a sad state of affairs when human innards are the tastier option over a school dinner. Definitely healthier though," I replied.

Hey don't judge me, hanging around with Dave was starting to rub off and besides, he was dealing with all of this a lot better than I was. Maybe if I took a leaf out of Dave's book and rolled with the punches I wouldn't be a jibbering mess with the world's worst gag reflex. I was wrong. The hungry school girl heard my not so quiet whisper and lifted her head out of the dead man's stomach to look directly at me. I knew her.

"Don't you fucking know how to be quiet?" Dave said, as he walked back to the car. *"Come on Kidda get in."*

"I know her," I replied, watching what used to be my daughter's best friend Jane Ellis stagger to her feet and jaggedly move towards me, intestines hanging from her mouth.

"You don't know her John you know who she used to be. This isn't that girl anymore," Dave said as he got back into the car and started the engine.

Jane and Emily had been best friends since infant school and I knew her family well. Peter and Kay Ellis are lovely people and have been very good to Emily and I over the years, even taking Emily on holiday with them on several occasions. Now their daughter was a zombie and quite taken with the idea of eating me.

I glanced over towards the bus and took another look at the kids piled up on top of each other. It was not the crash that killed them, but Jane. One of the kids had his throat ripped out and another had an arm torn from her body. I hadn't noticed this before but now it was as clear as the blue winter's sky.

"Get in the car John!" Dave shouted and I listened, doing as instructed.

"She did this. The bus, she caused all of this," I said, not taking my eyes from her.

"You might want to fasten your seat belt," Dave said revving the engine.

It was obvious what he was going to do and he was right. She couldn't be left to continue. How many other deaths would she be responsible for if we just drove away?

"Do it!" I exclaimed and with that, Dave put his foot down hard and the Thunderbird sped forward, smashing into Jane with force.

The impact pulled her body underneath the vehicle, which jerked up and down as it moved over her. Dave brought the car to a halt and we both turned to assess the damage behind us. Jane's body lay twisted and contorted, face down in the road. Her legs crushed and her right arm bent in a direction it should never have been subjected to. I felt sick to my stomach at what had become of this poor girl.

How was I going to tell Emily about this, and what of Jane's parents? Were they alive or had they met the same unfortunate fate as their daughter?

Jane lifted her head and looked directly at the car. With her one good arm she tried desperately to pull herself forward, gnawing her teeth. Dave put the car in reverse, the rear smashing into Jane's head, snapping it backwards and removing it clean from her body. We then watched as Jane's head rolled along the road.

So far we had killed three zombies and I had known all of them. All I wanted right now was my daughter.

Dave pulled up alongside the dead man that Jane had been scoffing. He was the bus driver. He stepped outside and knelt beside him, inspecting the name badge.

"Well Simon Choat," Dave said, reading the name, *"not the best way to go out lad but look on the bright side. This hell was over for you before it had really begun. It's the poor bastards like me and John here who are still alive that will suffer more. You got out easy kidda."*

Dave noticed a packet of cigarette's in the deceased bus driver's shirt pocket.

"Don't mind if I do!" he said, reaching down to retrieve the cigarettes, lighting one immediately.

"Right! Let's get a move on!" he added, getting back into the car.

"Dave, can I have a cigarette?" I asked, "If ever there was a time to take up smoking, I think this is it."

He lit a cigarette and passed it to me. I took a long pull on the cigarette and instantly threw up.

"Fuck sake lar the Thunderbird! Give me that." Dave yelled, snatching the cigarette out of my hand.

He now had two cigarettes and took a pull on them both at the same time.

"Fucking amateur," Dave said, as he started the car then turned left out of the way of the bus and continuing our journey to find Emily.

The drive to my daughter's school was horrifying. People ran screaming from their homes, followed closely by loved ones intent on eating them. People left their houses with bags of belongings, carrying them to their vehicles. Cars had been abandoned sporadically along the road. One car had come to a halt after mounting the curb and hitting a bus shelter. As we drove past we could see the driver hanging out of the opened car door, seatbelt still secured whilst his female passenger was tearing an ear from his head, chewing on it ravenously.

We drove under the Bridgewater Expressway Bridge leading onto Heath Road, hearing screaming as we passed underneath. I turned my head to see a man stood on the edge of the bridge looking at the road below, a zombie closely in pursuit. Taking suicide over being eaten alive, the man jumped to his death only to be followed by the zombie which fell from the bridge also, landing on top of its intended victim. The fall had inflicted considerable damage to the zombie's lower torso but this didn't stop it from using its arms and mouth to tear through the skin of its victim.

Dave turned the Thunderbird onto Latham Avenue where my daughter's school was located. It's a long road consisting mostly of houses situated on either side. Again, the scene was similar to our previous encounters. Chaos everywhere as people left their homes and packed up their vehicles. Where they were planning on going I did not know and I expect they didn't either. They just wanted out and who could blame them right? If I was in their position I would have been doing the exact same. Only I wasn't. I needed to find my daughter then get to my brother's house.

Dave manoeuvred the car between vehicles that were backing out into the road, ready to flee this hell infected town. The Grange Comprehensive School was positioned on the left hand side at the very top of the road and prior to that was the Grange Infants and Junior School. We could see the schools from our position then, directly ahead of us, two vehicles backed out of their driveways simultaneously from either side of the road and smashed into each other. Both drivers exited their cars and began screaming at each other, their petrified families watching on from inside the vehicles.

"Fucking Move!" Dave shouted whilst beeping the car horn.

The two guys in the street stopped arguing and instead turned their attentions to Dave and me.

"Nice one big mouth, this is just what we need," I said, making sure my passenger door was locked.

"Well it got them moving," Dave replied.

"Yes it did, towards us!" I yelled.

Just as it looked like we were going to have to fight the living as well as the dead, a small boy of no more than five years of age stumbled out from behind the vehicles in front and grabbed hold of one of the man's legs, biting into his calf. The man screamed in pain as he violently shook his leg, trying to free himself from the grip of the child zombie. The boy would not let go as he gnawed furiously on his flesh. The man slammed his leg with the boy attached against his car. After several slams the boy's grip was loosened and he let go of the man's torn and bloodied leg. Before the boy could get to his feet, the man viciously began stomping on him, breaking the skull and shattering the child's head, brains spraying out over his clothes and onto the floor. Whilst this was happening, the other man had walked back to his vehicle and retrieved a crowbar. No sooner had the bitten man killed the boy, the other man swung the crowbar with menace repeatedly whacking the bitten man in the head. The bitten man's family were hysterical in their car watching as their father and beloved husband was brutally murdered.

"He was bitten! I did you a favour," shouted the man with the crowbar at the bitten man's distraught family.

The man walked back to his car and drove away. In this harsh new world perhaps the man was right to do what he did. But in the way he did it? I'm not too sure.

Dave drove on, past the Grange Infant and Junior School. Small zombie children were wandering around the playground aimlessly. Several torn and shredded corpses of those eaten by the infected pupils littered the play area.

We arrived at the Grange Comprehensive. It was a big school with a substantial playground situated at the front of it. Surrounding the playground were iron gates used as security to keep would be vandals from the premises. Luckily for Dave and me, it was containing a hoard of teenage zombies from escaping.

We parked the Thunderbird outside the school gates and exited the vehicle, Dave taking his trusted battle paddle from the backseat. Zombie school kids pressed themselves up against the gates, gnashing their jaws and stretching their arms out in an attempt to grab us. Behind the zombies on the playground lay the remains of a dead teacher with two kids eating what was left of him. Well I assume it was a teacher. The only part of him that remained intact was his brown corduroy jacket with leather patches on the elbows. So it had to be a teacher right? Amongst the zombie kids were also zombie dinner ladies. One in particular caught my eye as she wandered around without direction, wearing a blood stained apron and chewing on a mutilated child's arm.

This wasn't looking good. If Emily was in there and alive, she must be hauled up somewhere but how the hell was I going to get in? I must have counted over forty zombies, possibly more. They had surrounded the school gates, making it impossible to climb over.

"Do you think there are zombies in there?" Dave said, looking at the school yard.

"Are you not seeing what I see?" I said, glaring at him.

"Well it's hard to tell. Every school looks like this to me" he replied, lighting another cigarette. *"It's not that bad Ace, I reckon we can figure out a way in no bother. How about, I'll distract the hungry fuckers while you climb over the gate and check out the school? If there's one thing going in our favour it's that these dead bastards are slow, not like your new and trendy Hollywood faster-is-better style zombies. As long as you get a head start you should be able to out run them. Here, you take this and wait for the path to clear. You'll be needing it more than me."*

Dave passed me his battle paddle and moved a good one hundred feet up the path that flanked the school gates. He began jumping around, waving his arms wildly and shouting at the zombies in an attempt to grab their attention.

"Hey you bunch of bastards look over here! There's enough of me to feed all of ya! Come and get your din dins ya ugly fuckers! Come on what's wrong? Lost your appetite? Hey fat lad, come and tuck in you know you want to. I'm tastier than that crap they serve you up for dinner. Hey dinner lady, put down that thin meatless arm you are chomping on and waddle over here. Let those flabby bingo wings grab a hold of something that's gonna fill you up. Grade A prime scouse over here kiddas ..."

Incredibly, Dave's plan was working. One by one the zombies slowly shuffled over to where he was throwing himself about like a teenage girl at a One Direction concert. With my area now zombie free, I threw the battle paddle over the gates and climbed over. I was in, and I was shitting myself. Dave couldn't help me now; it was all down to me.

With Emily as my motivation, I picked up the battle paddle and moved quickly towards the main entrance of the school. Not one of the zombies had noticed me. Instead they had crowded around the gate where Dave was putting on his one man show.

The main doors flung open and a large zombie kid stood in the doorway. I couldn't tell if he was fat before or if he was bloated from feasting on flesh. He was covered in blood from his mouth to his feet and it was fresh. This kid had eaten recently and he was hungry for seconds. I pushed the paddle hard into his stomach and his upper torso bent forward. I withdrew the paddle back, lifted it up high and brought it down swiftly on his head. It didn't put an end to his devilish existence but it did knock him to the ground. I turned the paddle around and with the pole shaped handle, began stabbing at his head over and over again until his skull caved and brain matter spread across the floor. That did it.

I stepped through the school's doors and realised I had no idea where I was going. Although this was the same school that I attended in the mid 90s, a lot had changed since then and the layout was considerably different. To the left of me were the remains of a child, ripped apart by zombies. Just beyond the kid, were two zombies, a man and a woman, and I assumed by their age and dress that they were teachers. Both of these zombies were dead, having had their heads completely destroyed. This gave me hope. There were people here that had weapons and knew how to defend themselves. I was just hoping that one of them would be my daughter.

"Emily!" I shouted, forgetting myself. I immediately regretted shouting as from around a corner came three

teenage zombies. Taking on one fat zombie was one thing but three? The battle paddle had proven effective in one on one combat but it was large and clumsy. I was going to struggle to dispose of three. Nether the less, there was no turning back. I was prepared to take on one hundred zombies if it meant finding my daughter.

The zombies slowly advanced, stumbling forward whilst gnawing and grabbing the air with their hands. The leader of the deadly trio was a boy of around fifteen years of age. His school uniform was gore stained and torn, slobber oozed from his revolting mouth and below the sweat and blood stained face, you could make out his terrible complexion. The poor kid. Not only did he wake up this morning with a face like a badly topped pizza but he turned into a zombie also. This kid's skin just couldn't catch a break.

I stabbed at his legs with the battle paddle knocking him to the ground then repeatedly clobbered his head until he was dead... again. No sooner had I put down the lead zombie, the other two were upon me. As I've said, Dave's paddle is great in one on one combat but when there is more than one zombie to kill, it's slow and clumsy and in this case was almost my downfall. I took a step backwards, attempting to put some distance from myself and the hungry devil children set on killing me, only my foot slipped in the brain mush of the zombie I had just exterminated and I fell to the floor, landing heavily on my back. It was agony as the pain radiated from my back and shot down my left leg. I knew what that meant. My back had gone, an old rugby injury from my teenage years had once again come back to haunt me. One of the zombies was right on top of me now and I lifted the paddle up straight, placing the shovel end in its undead chest. The paddle was the only thing stopping the zombie from falling on me and no doubt sending me to my death.

The smallest movement resulted in my back twinging, sending agonising shooting pains down my leg. I could barely move and holding off the zombie with the paddle was becoming increasingly difficult. Behind the devil kid, the other zombie approached, edging closer by the second, I had no idea how I was going to hold off two of the fuckers!

My paddle slipped from the zombie's chest and he fell on top of me. I pressed my hands against his chest in an attempt to keep his grotesque body away from mine and more importantly his mouth. His face moved inches from mine, rancid drool dripping from his mouth, landing on my cheek. And the smell! Oh man, I could almost taste his fetid breath as his teeth gnashed together just above my face. I was done for, of that I was sure. Holding this zombie away from biting my face was causing excruciating pain and the second zombie was only moments away. I was done, I could feel my hands and arms caving under the pressure and all I could think about was how I had failed my daughter. I closed my eyes, residing myself to death, pressure from holding the zombie easing from my arms as my body gave up.

Then I heard a noise. A heavy thud followed by a disgusting squelch and I could feel that the zombie was no longer on top of me. I opened my eyes to see a teenage boy holding a cricket bat drenched in blood. He was stood over a slaughtered zombie. I turned my head to see the back of a girl bent over another zombie, smashing it in the face with a hockey stick repeatedly. She girl turned to face me.

"*Dad?*" said Emily, slapping my face to bring me round, "*Dad! What are you doing here?*"

"*Holy shit that's your Dad,*" said the boy holding the cricket bat.

"*Come on help me, we've got to move him before more of these things turn up,*" she replied.

"*Emily, I saved you,*" I said, dizzy from the pain.

"*I think that should be the other way around Dad.*" Emily replied as her and the boy with the cricket bat carried me through a nearby door, laying me on a couch.

We were in the staff room and it was then that I blacked out.

The Battle for Poundland

It was 08:15am. Poundland had been open for fifteen minutes but not a soul had entered through the shop doors. Steven Pritchard would, on any other morning, be grateful for this as he could stand at the till gazing lustfully at Jess Smith, the girl who worked in the mobile phone shop directly opposite. He had spent many a morning stood at his till dreaming of the day he and Jess would finally hook up. Oh how happy they would be together. It was going to be a whirlwind romance, where he envisaged they would quickly marry, buy a house, have kids and live happily ever after. If only he could pluck up the courage to actually speak to her then she would fall in love with him, of that he was convinced. But for now, he was content to dream and admire Jess from the safety of his till, even if it did mean he had to watch whilst her slime ball of a boss Russell Ong flirted with her shamelessly. Not on this morning however, as the lights within the mobile phone shop stayed dark. This had struck him as unusual because although the shop didn't open for another forty five minutes, Jess could normally be seen getting things ready for customers.

With his regular morning pick me up not available, Steven turned to his mobile phone so he could log on to Facebook and read what his friends were getting up to. But his mobile data wasn't connecting to the network and boredom was quickly setting in. The only people he had seen that morning had been his manager Jo-Anne Burke and her sister and assistant Nikki Burke. The Sisters of

103

Doom as he had christened them due to the authoritarian regime they ran. The only other person he had seen was his friend and Halton Lea Shopping Centre security guard Tin Tin.

Halton Lea was a large shopping mall with its outside structure resembling a giant block of Lego. A product of early 1970s British architectural 'forward thinking' design, Halton Lea, under its original name of Runcorn Shopping City, had been officially opened by Queen Elizabeth II in 1972. At the time of its opening, Runcorn Shopping City was the largest enclosed shopping centre in Europe and attracted custom from all over the North West of England. 'The City' as known to Runcorn residents could not sustain its popularity, as the owners sought to capitalise on the initial success by increasing shop rents. This backfired, as many of the popular shops moved to the nearby town of Warrington where rent prices were low and demand was high. Now Halton Lea housed mostly discount stores, with Poundland being one of the most popular.

Steven hated quiet mornings as it gave him time to reflect on how miserable his life was and how dearly he wished for some excitement. He had worked for Poundland for coming up to ten years and at forty years of age, he was much older than the other employees. Poundland was meant to be a stop gap for him, something to do whilst he wrote his big screenplay, the one that would change his life forever. He spoke often about this; in fact he had been talking about it for almost fifteen years. No-one had read or even seen it and if they had it wouldn't take them long to get through the six pages he had written so far. He often pondered about when he would finally become a famous writer. Thinking about how talk show hosts would ask what he did prior to being a big name in Hollywood and how he would tell anecdotes about his time as a discount store worker, selling old people packets of Werther's Originals for £1. He would revel in telling stories of how he had risen from the checkout of Poundland to the bright lights of Los Angeles. The only thing he had risen from lately was his bed and even that had become a struggle of late. He felt his life was going nowhere and he longed for excitement. Silently fantasising about his would be life as a big shot Hollywood writer was no longer doing it for him and he needed something real.

As Steven lent against the till, resting his head in his hands and gazing at the closed mobile phone shop, a distant noise entered his ears. A croaking noise, almost prehistoric in its sound, echoed through the walkway of the shopping centre. He heard it again, only closer this time. Whatever made the sound was heading towards Poundland. He had initially assumed the owner of the noise was an animal of some sort; most likely a bird that had flown inside and was now looking for a way out. Then he saw him. A frail man, old in years, slowly stumbling in front of the Poundland window, dragging his bloodied and torn left leg along the floor as he moved. The old man stopped and turned to

Steven, pressing his thin pale face against the glass. The man groaned and began to thump his right fist against the window.

Steven's mouth opened, his jaw hanging low in both confusion and astonishment at what he was witnessing. Two thoughts entered his head. Get help or do nothing in the hope that the old man would simply just go away, and his conscience was battling with both. He knew the right thing to do would be to help the old man. He was clearly unwell and the leg injury alone was enough to warrant medical attention but the pale skin, glazed eyes and bloodied leg were all telling him to stay the fuck away.

He pressed the button that operates the shop tannoy system and spoke into the microphone next to his till.

"Jo-Anne or Nikki to the tills please."

The old man slid his body sideways along the window, making his way towards the shop entrance, his mouth leaving a trail of slobber as his face dragged against the glass. Steven spoke into the microphone again, this time with more of an urgent tone.

"Jo-Anne or Nikki to the tills please."

Still no response and by now, the man had made it into the entrance of Poundland and an unholy growl left his throat.

"Anyone to the fucking till please!" he yelled into the microphone.

Moving his good leg forward, the old man dragged himself forward. Steven was overcome with fear and his legs began to shake uncontrollably.

"Hello sir, can I interest you in some polo mints today? Two packs for £1?" he asked, his mind devoid of processing a sensible course of action.

Then, as if out of nowhere, Steven's friend and Halton Lea security guard Tin Tin, ran into the shop wielding a hammer and bludgeoned the old man across the back of the head. The force of the blow sent the old man to the ground and Tin Tin continued to pummel him. Steven found it difficult to find his voice, his mind unable to process what he was seeing. After what seemed to last forever, Tin Tin ended his assault, appearing satisfied with the destruction he had caused.

"Now stay dead you old bastard!" Tin Tin shouted, pointing his blood dripping hammer at the lumpy broth that used to be the old man's head. *"Close the shop door, don't let anyone in or out,"* he told Steven.

Steven in a state of shock at the horrifying could not respond.

"Earth to Steven, is there anyone there? I said close the door, we don't have any time to waste," he added.

"Yu, yu, you just killed that man," was his friends shaken, quiver toned response.

"No I didn't, he was already dead. I will take responsibility for turning his head into a goulash but killing him? No, whoever did that to his leg killed him," Tin Tin replied.

"What are you...? When? Who?" Steven asked.

"I see your vocabulary is still as great as always. If you can construct sentences as awesome as that, I can't wait to read the screenplay you've been telling me about for years. Steven, just do as I say and close the door. I'll get rid of granddad," Tin Tin replied.

Tin Tin grabbed the old man's legs and dragged him out of Poundland removing him from the shop doorway, leaving a slither of blood and head matter on the floor in doing so.

"What the hell is going on?" Steven asked.

"Zombies my friend, zombies," Tin Tin informed whilst rifling through the dead man's pockets and pulling out a bus pass. "Sorry Mr Christopher Lyons," he said, reading the name on the pass. "It was either you or me. Steven, I don't want to ask again, please can you close the shop door?"

"I can't Tin Tin, only the manager and assistant manager have keys and I haven't seen them since I came in," Steven replied.

"Well where are they now?" Tin Tin asked.

"In the store room out the back. They were both complaining of feeling unwell," Steven answered.

"How do you mean unwell? How did they look?" Tin Tin pressed.

"Terrible. They were sweating badly and suffering with stomach cramps. Why?" Steven asked.

"Grab yourself something you can use as a weapon, something strong enough to crack a skull," Tin Tin told Steven.

"Tin Tin, zombies? Are you sure? Do you realise how ridiculous that sounds?" said Steven.

Tin Tin walked outside of Poundland and looked up and down the shopping mall walkway.

"Come here," he asked of Steven, who followed him to the walkway, carefully avoiding the blood and brain juice on the floor.

"Now do you believe me?" he asked, directing Steven's attention to the oncoming threat.

Steven looked left and straight away wished he was back home having never risen from his bed. Staggering towards him some 50ft away shuffled five figures, faces hidden due to their stooped posture. He knew on first sight that Tin Tin was right.

"Fuck me," was Steven's response. *"We need to get those keys for the door."*

Then, a large groan was heard resonating throughout Poundland. Steven and Tin Tin immediately turned their attentions from the oncoming zombies to the noise within the store.

"I best get a weapon," Steven said.

"Is there some kind of delayed reaction going on with you today? Stop repeating what I asked of you a few minutes ago and get a move on. You grab a weapon and check on what made that noise. If it came from your manager, bash her head in and take the keys. I'll make the front of the shop as secure as I can" Tin Tin replied.

Steven ran to the gardening aisle of Poundland and ripped open the packaging on two handheld digging forks. Used for planting, he surmised that the forks would be more than capable of penetrating the skull of a zombie. Just to make sure, he swooshed a few practice swings.

Thump!

Steven heard the noise of something or someone banging against the storeroom doors. The doors were heavy duty, double acting saloon doors but with a little force they could be easily pushed open.

Thump! Thump!

Steven, with his newly assigned weaponry at hand, moved towards the storeroom doors to investigate. He pushed his face up against the Perspex window of one of the doors and almost immediately the undead face of Jo-Anne, his manager, pressed up against the other side. Behind her, also visible through the window, was her sister Nikki. He grabbed a broom and placed in through the handles of both doors, securing the Sisters of Doom in the storeroom... for now.

Whilst Steven was assigning himself weapons and dealing with his bosses, Tin Tin was collecting as many bottles of shower gel as he could then emptying them out on the walkway directly outside the entrance, creating a river of slippery fluid. By the time he was satisfied with his slimy creation, the oncoming zombies were a mere 10ft away.

"Steven!" Tin Tin called.

Steven was looking into the cold dead eyes of his boss through the Perspex window of the storeroom door when he heard the call. Jo-Anne's mouth oozed with saliva as she bared her teeth, gnarling at the window.

"Coming," Steven replied, turning away from his flesh hungry manager.

"When they fall, smash their fucking heads in," Tin Tin instructed. *"Good choice in weaponry by the way. Did you happen to see what made that noise?"*

"Yep," Steven replied.

"Zombies?" Tin Tin asked.

"Yep, Jo-Anne and Nikki but I've locked them in the storeroom. I didn't fancy taking on both of them on my own." Steven replied.

"We'll deal with them soon enough, but these bastards need sorting out first. Get ready," Tin Tin said, gripping his blood stained hammer.

The first of the zombies, a female, lumbered forward. As its foot hit the slippery river of shower gel, it slid forward falling heavily. The zombie began to move from side to side, slipping and sliding in the shower gel, unable to rise to its feet.

"Put these on," Tin Tin instructed, passing Steven a child's pair of pink Hello Kitty wellington boots.

"Why do I have to wear pink ones? You've got green ones, why can't I wear green too?" Steven asked upset with the choice Tin Tin had made for him.

"Because, tiddly toes, you have the foot size of an eight year old girl and these are the only ones Poundland had in

your size," Tin Tin explained. *"Don't blame me because you have feet a baby would be ashamed of."*

Tin Tin placed his feet inside the green wellington boots and walked out into the river of shower gel. With one fast swing, he drove his hammer into the forehead of the zombie, ending her undead existence instantly. He reached into her jacket pocket and retrieved her purse, opening it to ascertain her identity.

"Tracey Oldfield, sorry for smashing your brains in but hey, needs must. That's 2 – 0 to me now mate, you can kill the next one, it'll give you a chance to catch up." Tin Tin said.

The second and third zombies arrived together and again they were female. Slipping almost simultaneously, they both fell to the floor. Steven removed his shoes and slipped his dainty size 4s into the child's Hello Kitty wellingtons and, to his annoyance, they were a perfect fit. He waded his way through the shower gel and looked down at the fallen undead as they reached up grabbing at his feet.

"Well, Steven, you wanted excitement!" he said to himself, before stabbing both zombies in the head with his gardening forks.

"2:2," he said, turning to face Tin Tin, who nodded at him approvingly.

Steven didn't need to search their dead bodies for identification as he knew who they were.

"That's Julia Kelly and Niki Kelly, sisters that worked in the betting shop next door. They used to come in every morning before work to buy milk and biscuits and I just killed them," he said.

"They were dead already mate. Just keep telling yourself you didn't kill them; they were dead already. You did good, I'm proud of you. I'll take the next one but we really need to get the keys from your boss so we can close this door before more arrive. Shower gel won't hold them off forever." Tin Tin said.

"Well I've secured the storeroom, so the Sisters of Doom won't be going anywhere soon," Steven informed.

Steven had barely finished his sentence when a sharp snapping sound followed by the noise of the heavy storeroom doors opening filled the air. The wooden broom handle Steven had used to secure the doors had broken due to the pressure from Jo-Anne and Nikki continually pushing against it.

"Damn those cheap ass Poundland products!" Steven moaned.

Steven and Tin Tin turned their heads towards the shop and from the back, next to the baby section, stumbled into view the Sisters of Doom. Tin Tin turned his gaze back towards the fourth zombie, which was slowly heading to their location. He wasn't going to wait for him to arrive at the shower gel lake, not with the Sisters of Doom approaching. He walked out towards the undead, careful to avoid the slippery floor and thrust his hammer through the air cracking the zombie on its forehead. The zombie's head fractured on contact, spraying blood and gore over the window of Card Factory, a nearby discount greeting card store.

"Hammer Time," Tin Tin smirked.

"Did you just make a pun?" Steven asked.

"Fucking right I did!" Tin Tin proudly stated whilst looking through the dead zombie's wallet, finding the man's name on an ID card. *"Mr Peter Sariwee has over £200 here. I'll take that thank you. Now then Steven, let's go and sort out the Sisters of Doom before the other zombie gets here."*

Steven and Tin Tin walked back into Poundland, approaching the Sisters of Doom as they staggered down the baby product isle.

"There," Steven said, pointing towards the keys that were attached to a chain, hanging from Jo-Anne's trouser waist.

The Sisters of Doom shuffled slowly forward, their sweat and puke stained clothes hanging heavily from their frames as they swayed from side to side, knocking various products from shelving units.

"I'll take boss lady," Tin Tin announced, pointing at Jo-Anne as gloops of saliva dripped from her quickly decaying mouth.

"No way, she's mine. This bitch has made my life hell too often and for too long. No mate, I'm doing it," Steven said with purpose.

"Be my guest but do it quickly, we don't have much time. I'll take out Deputy Doom," Tin Tin replied, pointing at Nikki.

Tin Tin marched towards his target and with one ferocious swing, smashed his hammer into the side of her face, shattering her jaw and sending teeth flying from her mouth. He swung again, this time cracking the hammer against the side of her head, sending her soaring into the shelving units. He hunched over her fallen body, repeatedly bringing the hammer down onto her head, time and time again, turning her undead body back to plain old dead.

Having watched Tin Tin destroy Deputy Doom, adrenalin started to pump through Steven's veins. His new found assertiveness in the face of the apocalypse was having a startling effect and for the first time in his life, he felt alive. He finally had a purpose and as basic as it seemed, staying alive was now his only priority. It was time to take down the boss. With gardening forks held tightly in both hands, he raised his arms above his head and lunged at Jo-Anne, stabbing her through the top of the head with both forks. She died instantly, collapsing in a heap on the ground, the forks sticking out of her head like a pair of novelty antlers.

"Fork you Jo-Anne!" Steven screamed.

"Very good," Tin Tin said, approving of Steven's one liner. *"Grab the keys and help me take the Sisters of Doom out to the front of the shop. We don't need these two stinking the place up now do we? Once we have secured the entrance, I reckon we should empty some shelving units and place them in front of the window. Pretty soon this place is going to be crawling with zombies and those units will help reinforce the window. We could have a hundred or so pressed up against the glass trying to get at us. The shelving units will add some much needed protection."*

Steven agreed and together, they removed the Sisters of Doom from Poundland, dumping their bodies in the river of shower gel along with the other fallen undead.

Using the keys he took from Jo-Anne, Steven closed the doors to the store, securing both himself and Tin Tin inside whilst the latter began to empty shelving units, ready to be used to reinforce the windows.

Just as he was about to walk away from the doors to help Tin Tin, he noticed the light come on in the mobile phone shop opposite. It was Jess Smith and she wasn't alone. Jess had entered the shop in a hurry and in some distress as she slouched over the shop counter, holding her right arm to apply pressure to a visibly bloodied open wound. Due to her stress, she hadn't noticed the stooped figure stood behind her. Steven had though and he started to manically bang on the door to Poundland, shouting her name in an attempt to alert her to the danger behind her but it was no good, his cries, like his love for her, went unnoticed.

"Jess! JESS! Hey!" he screamed, banging on the glass as hard as he could.

The stooped figure lifted his head and moved slowly forward towards her. It was her boss Russell Ong. His movement alerted her to his presence and she turned to face him. The fear in her face was evident as she backed away, begging him to stop his advances. She looked around for something she could use to protect herself. With her good arm, she grabbed display phone after display phone, throwing them at him in quick succession but it had little effect. He was hungry and it was going to take more than a Nokia Lumia to the head to crush his need to feed.

She desperately scanned the shop for something more substantial to use. She reached for an iPad then ran at Russell, powerfully jamming it into his mouth with all the strength she could muster. The impact was such that both sides of his pale dead lips split and the iPad lodged between his jaws but still he stalked his prey, following her as she walked with her back to the walls continuing to throw as many phones at him as she could. She found herself back at the counter with nowhere else to go and Russell almost upon her. With both hands she lifted the shop till above her head and with as much force as she could, brought it crashing down on his head. Finally he stopped, lying in a heap of blood and smartphones. Relieved and exhausted, she collapsed on the floor; her head slouched forward with her back leaning against the counter.

Steven witnessed it all and felt relief that Jess was at least safe from the zombie that used to be her boss. He moved to open the doors to Poundland. She needed assistance and he couldn't just leave her there, not the woman he loved. Before he could place the key in the lock, Tin Tin snatched them from his hand.

"Bad idea Steven," he said.

"Look at her, she's hurt. We can help her. I'll be in and out in no time, just give back the keys," Steven replied.

"She's more than hurt, she's infected. There's nothing we can do," Tin Tin informed solemnly, placing his hand on Steven's shoulder for comfort.

Steven looked across to Jess, longing to be with her. He desperately wanted Tin Tin to be wrong but he had seen her wound and he knew it to be true. He watched as her body began to jolt and vomit leaked from her mouth. She quickly went into spasm, shaking feverishly for several seconds as if a thousand volts of electricity shot through her body. Then nothing, she was still, her body limp and lifeless on the floor. Steven felt numb. Resting his head against the window, a tear rolled down his cheek as he looked upon the woman he loved.

"Come on mate, help me with the shelving units, there's nothing you could have done," said Tin Tin.

Steven lowered his head and took a deep breath. Tin Tin was right of course, there was nothing he could have done to help but that did nothing to ease the pain. He wiped the lonely tear from his cheek and lifted his head to offer one last look to Jess. What awaited his eyes sent a cold chill through his spine. She was now stood upright and pressed up to the window of the mobile phone shop, slapping her left hand against the glass repeatedly. Her cold dead eyes had, for the first time in her life, noticed Steven and she was longing for him but not in a way he had ever imagined.

Steven pressed his right hand against the window and mouthed *'goodbye'* to Jess before turning to help his friend secure the shop.

It was the start of what was going to be a very long day.

Journal Entry 4

I slowly opened my eyes. The blurred image of my daughter filling my sight only helped to confuse my already weary mind. I had no idea where I was or what was happening.

"Dad, you're awake!" said Emily eagerly.

"Thunderbirds," I replied, the pain from my back restricting my ability to communicate properly.

"I think your Dad's lost it," said the boy with the cricket bat.

"Gary Numan in a Thunderbird," I continued.

"Definitely lost it," he said again.

"Sorry Dad," Emily said apologetically before slapping me hard across the face.

That did the trick as I snapped out of my haziness and hurtled back into reality.

The room I was in was spacious and I had been placed on a couch surrounded by large chairs and a television set. The TV was turned on but nothing was broadcasting. There was another girl in the room. She was sat directly in front of the TV flicking through every channel. They all broadcasted the same message.

'This channel is currently unavailable.'

"Oh my actual God, can you believe that the television is like so totally lame. There is nothing on what-so-ever! Even the channel Dave has stopped running repeats of Top Gear. We are all like, totally doomed." Said the girl.

Everything she wore was black. Black shoes, black jeans, black hoody, black lipstick, black fingernails, black hair, black…. Well, you get the picture. And to compliment all of the blackness, she had a complexion that made zombies look like they have just come back from sunning themselves for two weeks in Magaluf.

"She's happy isn't she?" I said sarcastically to Emily.

"Dad, this is my friend, Louise Brown. She's a Goth," Emily replied.

Louise turned her head from the television and looked at me.

"We are all going to die," she said, then turned her head back to the television and continued flicking through the channels.

It's the end of the world and I was trapped in a room with a back that was refusing to work and the world's most depressed teenager. Perfect! But at least I had found my daughter.

There was a man in the room also, washing dishes in the kitchen area of the staff room. He was in his mid to late fifties. He was sporting a moustache and the greatest cardigan you have ever seen - the kind that would make Starsky & Hutch jealous.

"Where are we? Emily thank God you're safe. If I could move I'd hug you," I said through gritted teeth, tight pulling pains running up by back as I attempted to adjust my position.

"We're in the staff room at school. We managed to secure it once we realised what was going on. How did you get here Dad? I've been worrying about you. We found you almost passed out in the hallway with a zombie on top of you. You were nearly dead." Emily said with concern in her eyes.

"I'm with my friend Dave, he's outside putting on a song and dance routine to distract the zombies in the playground. We need to get out of here, it's not safe, this place is surrounded," I said, trying to sit up.

"Oh I think you'll find that we're quite secure here Mr Diant. There is only one way in and that door is locked. We have running water, electricity, toilets over there next to a fully stocked vending machine, milk in the fridge and food in the cupboards. As you can see we even have a television set. I think we'll be fine here till it all blows over. Cup of tea Mr Diant?" asked the man with the Moustache as he filled the kettle with water.

"Who the hell is this moron?" I asked.

"That's Mr Kelly, he's the Headmaster of the school," Emily replied.

"Please Mr Diant, you can call me Robert or Rob. My friends call me Rob," said Emily's headmaster.

"Ok Robert. Do you really think this room will keep you safe? That this thing will just blow over and the world will go back to normal? You should take a look outside. Society has quite quickly turned to shit. Not half a mile from here I've seen people kill each other trying to get away from this thing. Just to get here, my friend and I have killed 3 zombies and as people, I knew all of them. How long do you think you're little vending machine will stay full? And what will happen when the electricity fails, which it will? And the water you're using, how long will it be fit to drink? How do you know this thing didn't start from the water supply? If you're happy to stay in this room, like a rat in a trap, then that's fine with me, but I say we get out of here." I replied, slightly more defensive than maybe I should have been but this guy was a stiff and I was in too much pain to tolerate him.

"Darren Pickstock," Mr Kelly said sternly.

"What's he banging on about?" I asked Emily, who did not reply, instead she lowered her head, looking at the floor.

"Suzanne Jackson, Alison Knox, Paul Turner…" Mr Kelly continued.

It became clear what Mr Kelly was doing. It had perhaps been rather presumptuous off me to assume that Dave and I were the only two that had suffered.

"Paula Louise Wain, Katie Davis, Ashleigh White and her sisters Jessica White and Louisa White..." he continued.

Mr Kelly was unrelenting with his name listing. My daughter kept her eyes firmly fixed on the ground. Even the Goth girl stopped flicking through TV channels.

"Melanie Baker-Owen, Kathryn Gill, should I continue Mr Diant?" said Mr Kelly.

Man I felt like I was back in school being told off for talking during an exam. I had made a massive mistake in mouthing off like that and I was being firmly put in my place and in front of my daughter too.

"There are over one thousand students in this school. Do you know how many I know by name? Every single one of them. You're not the only person to have suffered Mr Daint," Mr Kelly replied. *"How do you think we came to secure this room? Luck? We have lost many children, teachers, dinner ladies, classroom assistants and office staff over the last few hours. Your situation is not unique,"* he said.

"Look I'm sorry. I shouldn't have said what I said. I was wrong," I replied sheepishly. *"Emily I'm sorry, I, I didn't think,"* I said to my daughter.

"It was horrible Dad. I was in PE…" Emily began.

"Oh my God it was like the worst PE class EVER! Hockey, I mean, can you believe it?" Louise added turning to face us for a second before returning to flicking through the television channels, her eyes just visible from behind her long dark fringe.

"Louise you don't like doing any kind of sport," Emily replied. *"Anyway, thank God it was hockey or you wouldn't be alive now. We were playing hockey in the sports hall because Mr Bignall had said it was too cold to play on the field and he wasn't feeling too good and that we should all keep warm."*

"Mr Bignall, or Mike as he was better known to me. He was a good teacher," Mr Kelly interjected.

"Was?" I asked.

I had a feeling I knew how this story was going.

"We were all playing hockey… well, I say all. We had to play five a side because not everyone had turned up which was strange. Even my friend Jane hadn't come to school and she's never off sick," Emily said.

I didn't have the heart to tell her the reason Jane never made it to school was because she turned into a zombie on the bus ride in, murdered a bunch of other school kids and ate the bus driver. Oh, and we killed her by removing her head!

"Mr Bignall was refereeing. Well, he was supposed to but he was too busy being ill. He kept excusing himself and running outside. He wasn't the only one either. Five aside hockey turned into three aside hockey because people kept throwing up. Then I noticed that Mr Bignall looked different. His skin had turned a whitish grey and his face was full of veins. He staggered back into the sports hall and flung his arms around Hannah Burgess, dragging her to the floor. I hadn't noticed at first but as soon as she started screaming I ran over. He was ripping the skin from her face like a child opening Christmas presents. It was horrible Dad. The others ran for the exit in fear but the kids that had been throwing up had blocked the doorway. One off them, Paula Gilsenan, had the same pale complexion as Mr Bignall and she reached out to Steph Verney, grabbing her leg and biting into her calf muscle. Then the other sick kids dove on top of her. They ripped her stomach open and guzzled her insides like they hadn't eaten a meal for a week," Emily explained, her voice shaking as she recalled the horrific events._

"We were trapped in the sports hall with what we now know to be zombies blocking our way out and Mr Bignalll munching his way through my friend Hannah. I took my hockey stick and I bashed him over the head with it again and again until he was dead. Well, dead again. Can zombies die twice? Anyway, I killed him and then I grabbed Louise who was crying in a corner..."_

"Hey hold on Emily, I wasn't crying, that would be like so lame. I had something in my eye ok," Louise interrupted.

"Well, whatever, I grabbed Louise and we fought our way out of the sports hall, killing Paula Gilsenan, then running out of the door. It was just after that that we found Jonathon." Emily continued, pointing at the boy guarding the door.

"Hi, I'm your daughter's er, your daughter's friend, pleasure to meet you," Jonathon said, his arm outstretched to shake my hand.

I didn't return the gesture. To be honest, I didn't like the look of him and I wasn't buying for one second that he was just my daughter's 'friend'.

"He's your friend?" I asked Emily in disbelief, who nodded in reply without making eye contact. "But he's wearing skinny jeans? And look at his long hair; he looks like he spends more time brushing it than you do with yours."

"Dad if it wasn't for Jonathon I might not be alive right now," Emily added.

"Oh Jonathon, you're my hero!" Louise added, fluttering her eyelids, mocking Emily.

"Shut up Louise," Emily blushed, shoving her friend.

"Louise and I left the sports hall and oh my God Dad it was awful. There were kids screaming and running everywhere.

128

I just wanted to go home and the most direct route would be to leave through the school's front entrance and across the car park. Only, blocking our path was Mr Barton and Miss Rimmer. Well, what used to be Mr Barton and Miss Rimmer. They were both shredding apart a year 8 student like a tear and share garlic bread," Emily informed.

She's always had a way with describing things. She's the only person I know that can inform you of someone being eaten alive and make you hungry for Italian food at the same time.

"Paul Barton. Another good teacher lost and a bloody great friend too. Then there's Lisa Rimmer, our newest member of staff. Such a shame," Mr Kelly added.

"Last in first out eh?" I said.

Everyone looked at me appalled at what was, without question, a terrible joke.

"Sorry about that, my brain and my mouth aren't always connected and I'm prone to inappropriate outbursts during stressful situations. It's a family thing but luckily for Emily here, it appears to have passed her by. If you think I'm bad you should meet my brother and I'm rambling now so I'll shut up. Again, I'm sorry."

I really needed to get some pain killers!

"Do you often make fun of the dead Mr Diant?" Mr Kelly asked.

Again, he made me feel like I was back in school. I thought it best not to answer and instead lowered my head in shame.

"So the only thing between us and the exit was Mr Barton and Miss Rimmer. I had already taken out two zombies but not two at the same time. Luckily for me I didn't have to because just as my two former teachers noticed both Louise and me, Jonathon appeared and took them out with his cricket bat," Emily said.

"They had a good inning," Jonathon said, tapping his cricket bat on the floor then performing a mock swing.

"Nice, I see what you did there," I said, approving of his dry humour.

I still wasn't keen on the kid though. Any kid that introduces himself as my daughter's *"friend"* but is clearly more will have to work harder than that to win me over. Yes I know he saved Emily's life but what can I say? I'm a hard man to please.

"Jonathon Buckley, I've told Mr Diant and now I'm telling you. Do not make fun of the dead. These people were your peers, show some respect!" said Mr Kelly, also giving Jonathon a stern telling off.

"It wasn't too difficult really. The back of Mr Barton's head completely caved in after one shot but Miss Rimmer took a

couple of beatings before she went down." Jonathon added, ignoring Mr Kelly.

He was slowly growing on me.

"Jonathon!" Mr Kelly yelled, slamming his fist down on the table unit in the kitchen area.

"So, Jonathon saved both me and Louise and took us to the staff room for safety. Mr Kelly was already here. As far as we know this is it. Everyone else is either dead or a zombie," said Emily.

We couldn't stay here. Yes the staff room was secure for now but how long would that last? There was one way in and one way out. The door Jonathon was guarding was already coming under pressure by the banging of zombies stumbling against it. It wouldn't hold out forever and what of 80s Dave? I couldn't leave him outside, alone. Not after everything he had done for me.

"We can't stay here. That door won't hold out forever. You know that noise you can hear? That thudding up against the door? It will only get worse. More and more of them will come when they realise we're in here and when that door finally gives out, what then? What's the plan? Because from what I see we have nowhere to go. Our best bet is to leave now while we still stand a chance," I said.

"My Dad is right. We need to leave. It's our best chance. We should go to Uncle Butty's place. He'll know what to do," Emily added.

"I am the head master of the school and I say we stay here. It's our best chance of surviving until the police or the army get here and sort out this mess. As for you saying this door isn't secure... utter nonsense! These doors are as solid as the foundations of this school." Mr Kelly said, whilst marching over to the staff room door and banging on it in a demonstration of how sturdy it was.

"See, nothing is getting through this door, nothing," was to be Mr Robert Kelly's last sentence.

Well, as long as you discount his screams as two flesh shredded arms came smashing through the door, grabbing him by the throat and snapping his neck.

The zombie held on to Mr Kelly, as it forced its head through the newly made hole in the door.

"Holly shit that's Simon Dooley. Oh man Mr Kelly hated him, he suspended him from school twice for flashing Miss Rimmer," Jonathon said.

Louise screamed and dove behind the television as we watched Simon Dooley strain his head through the hole in the door and rip an ear clean from Mr Kelly's head. Well, if there was one thing to get me moving, it was that! It's funny how easily you can forget about pain when you're about to shit yourself. I jumped to my feet, grabbed Emily's hockey stick and repeatedly jabbed at the zombie's forehead; breaking skin, then skull, then finally brain.

"Ouch!" I whimpered as my posture stiffened with the swift return of back pain.

Emily helped me back to the sofa whilst Jonathon moved a cabinet in front of the now broken door. Louise? She was still crying behind the television.

"Well that settles it, now we have to leave," I said through gritted teeth.

"I'm with you Mr Diant, we need to get moving. It won't take long for the zombies to realise we're here now." Jonathon said.

"My friend is outside with a car. If we can get to him, we can go to my brother's house. We'll be safe there, trust me, he's been looking forward to this day his whole life. Emily do you think you can stop your friend from crying? That kind of noise will only attract unwanted attention." I said.

Whilst Emily comforted Louise, I painfully rose to my feet. This wasn't going to be easy but we had been compromised and now leaving was the only option. Luckily for me, I had Emily and her, ahem, 'friend' Jonathon. I just hoped we could make it to 80s Dave and that he was safe.

Duck for Cover

Becky Brake could not remember a time when she had ever been so ill. Her entire body hurt from the smallest of movements. A slight tilt of the head gave a migraine so powerful she felt like someone had lit a fire within her brain. Stillness was unfortunately not an option, as illness brought with it sickness and Becky had spent the majority of the night hugging the toilet, projectile vomiting preventing any chance of rest. During moments when sickness eased and she was afforded some much needed rest, she would turn to her mobile phone wearily. Her tear soaked eyes strained to see the small clock in the centre of the glass screen and desperately she begged for time to speed up, for it to be 6.30am when her husband Phil would be home from work. The one thing Becky was thankful for was her baby daughter Gaby who, at ten weeks old, was a brilliant sleeper and had remained snoozing since before the onset of her sickness. The small amount of strength Becky could muster was being used to hold on to the toilet; she wasn't sure if she possessed the energy to tend to her daughter should she require comforting or need her nappy changing. She was also fearful that this sickness could be contagious and should she pass this on to her baby, Gaby would not have the strength to recover from something so severe. Becky could never forgive herself if something happened to her children.

Becky's oldest daughter Sophie could hear her mother's moans and had wanted to leave the comfort of her bedroom to help but Teddy had become poorly also and she dare not leave him. Teddy was Sophie's best friend and he had barely left her side since her father gave him to her shortly after she was born seven years ago. Teddy had been there for everything. Sophie's first words, her first steps… she loved him dearly and now he needed her to be there for him.

Phil was tired and it was with grateful relief that he finally placed his key in the door to the home he shared with his wife and two daughters. It had been a long and difficult shift, made even harder by the bug that had struck over half of the warehouse staff, leaving Phil to do the majority of the work on his own. He was a forklift truck driver for a large pharmaceutical company and had not had a day off since his paternity leave finished following the birth of Gaby. Times had been tough for the Brakes, and Phil had taken every opportunity to work all of the overtime available the past 2 months, meaning he had spent very little time with his family, but not today. Phil had been looking forward to today for a long time. Not only was it the wedding of his good friends Wesley and Heather, but for the first time in several months, he would get to spend time with his family. All he needed was a few hours rest to recharge his batteries and he would be good to go.

Phil had not taken two steps into his hallway when he heard the retching and moaning coming from the bathroom at the top of his stairs.

"Phil!"

He heard Becky cry his name and he deflated, knowing very well that rest was now out of the equation.

"Coming."

With heavy strides, he slowly walked up his staircase, the bathroom becoming more visible with every step.

The door to the bathroom was open. The bright light difficult on his eyes as he approached from the dark stairway. When his eyes adjusted the first thing he noticed was how disgusting the wooden floor in his bathroom was. Large gloops of sticky brown and green fluid covered the solid oak flooring. Phil couldn't make out what it was at first, then the smell of puke hit his nostrils and he gagged, almost adding his own contribution to the vomitorium that was once his bathroom. The first thought he had was one of despair. He had spent a full day laying that surface after Becky had insisted on having real wooden flooring. He would have been happy with laminate as it was cheaper and looking at his flooring now, it would almost definitely cope better with pools of acidy barf.

Beyond Phil's ruined flooring lay his wife, Becky. She clung to the toilet like her life depended on it. Phil's despair over his precious floor subsided quickly when he saw how ill she looked.

"I was aiming for the toilet," Becky whimpered.

She looked frail, her head, too heavy for her neck, swayed slightly as she struggled to lift it from the toilet seat. Phil looked at his boots apologetically then entered the bathroom to comfort his wife.

"How long have you been like this?" he asked, pulling the sweat soaked hair out of her pale, tortured face.

"Too long. I've been texting you, didn't you get any of my messages?" Becky replied, pausing mid-sentence to empty her mouth of excess saliva.

"No my phone isn't working, I haven't been able to get a signal all night. You need a doctor, I'll get one out on call." He replied as he made to leave the bathroom to retrieve the landline telephone.

"No I'll be fine really, I just need to rest. I don't need a doctor," Becky said.

Becky was a nurse and to Phil, that made her more qualified than him on matters of illness. So against his better judgement, he did not call for a doctor. Instead he brought her water, painkillers and a sick bucket then helped her to their bedroom so she could try to rest.

Phil gently lifted baby Gaby from her crib and placed her in a Moses basket then carried her to Sophie's bedroom. He looked over to Sophie, who was snuggling Teddy and doing a brilliant job at pretending to be asleep. Becky had told him how Gaby had been an angel and slept soundly but she was soon due a feed and he wanted to clean the bathroom first to save his wooden flooring.

Sophie heard her bedroom door close and marginally opened her eyes. All clear. Daddy hadn't noticed she was pretending to be asleep and she could once again tend to Teddy who was still unwell.

After cleaning the bathroom the best he could, he gave Gaby her feed then prepared breakfast for Sophie, which consisted of a croissant and a bowl of Coco Pops; her favourite. Phil's breakfast? Three large mugs of strong coffee. He had endured a long night and knew an even longer day lay in waiting. His wife, Becky, would be too ill to go to Heather and Wesley's wedding, of that he was certain. This meant it would be just him and the children, something he wasn't looking forward to. With no sleep, he wasn't sure how he was going to cope. Thankfully, Gaby had gone straight back to sleep after her feed and he afforded himself a few minutes shut eye at the kitchen table. It may have been longer had Sophie not appeared through the doorway.

"Morning Daddy, is it time for breakfast?" Sophie asked, clutching Teddy closely as she walked into the kitchen, sitting opposite her father at the table.

Phil jolted from his snooze and smiled at Sophie lovingly before pouring milk on her Coco Pops.

"Is mummy ok?" Sophie asked, tucking into her cereal.

"She's ok sweetheart. Mummy's just a little poorly that's all," he replied.

"Teddy's poorly too. Do you know what he said would make him better? If we could go and feed the duckies after breakfast," said Sophie.

As tired as he was, Phil thought this to be a good idea. It would clear his head and give Becky some much needed peace and quiet.

"Well if Teddy thinks it will make him better, then we better do as he says hadn't we? Eat your breakfast and get yourself dressed, then we'll go and feed the ducks," he replied.

The cold air was a relief to Phil's tired face as he pushed Gaby in her pram along Mersey road heading towards the grass embankment that overlooked the Manchester ship canal and the River Mersey. This was home to many wild ducks and geese and Sophie loved feeding them, especially the geese, as they would surround her and take pieces of bread directly from her hands. Geese, ducks... they were all duckies to Sophie and she skipped alongside her father, Teddy in one hand and a loaf of bread in the other.

It had been a strange early morning walk to Mersey road. For a Monday morning and closing in on 8am, he had expected to see more traffic. Instead there was nothing. The only cars he had noticed were parked, albeit erratically. He had barely seen a soul either. He had thought he'd seen the occasional person but they were always at a distance and it was hard to tell. There was a figure that looked to be slowly walking along the canal and he had sworn he had seen someone stood in a doorway of Swimming Pool, but he couldn't be sure. There had been nobody else though, until now.

Phil slowed down and took Sophie by the arm to prevent her from walking onward. Ahead in the road, in the small parking area that looked over the embankment of the Manchester Ship Canal and River Mersey, was a crowd of ducks and geese. They were fighting each other over whatever was in the middle of the huddle they had formed. Aggressive quacks echoed along the empty street and feathers flew into the air.

"They look hungry Daddy," said Sophie innocently.

"Yes they do don't they?" he replied, *"Can you do me a big favour sweetheart and just wait here and look after your little sister? I'll be right back."*

He cautiously walked towards the duck and geese gathering. Curiosity had gotten the better of him and he wanted to know what was in the centre of the feathered mosh pit, causing them to act so wildly. As he got closer, he at first noticed a trainer and then an exposed leg, frozen and pale blue in colour. It was an adult body, male and by the frost covered skin, it had been there for some time. The ducks and geese were pecking away at the man,

141

ripping flesh and covering the body in bloodied lesions and welts. Then the man's face became visible. Even with the open sores and frozen skin he knew who it was. The man was Barrie Jones, an old school friend and someone he was looking forward to seeing later at Heather and Wesley's wedding.

Phil puked instantly; the sight of his fallen friend was too much for him to take. The retching noise that accompanied his vomiting drew the attention of the smaller ducks that were having little luck pecking the body due to the larger geese bullying their way to the front. The ducks started to waddle towards him, quacking and rustling their feathers feverishly. The closest of the ducks, flapped its wings and started to fly just above ground level, directly at Phil, who swatted it away with his hands as it approached. The duck tumbled across the road then quickly got to its feet and waddled back to him, quacking like a creature possessed. He wasn't messing about this time and booted the duck hard in its chest, propelling it down the embankment towards the Manchester Ship Canal.

One by one the crazed ducks came and one by one Phil took them out. Kicks, punches, shoves and throws. He did whatever was needed to keep the feathered crazies away from him and more importantly his daughters. Sophie held on to Teddy, confused and terrified at the scene in front of her.

With all the ducks disposed of, only geese remained and unluckily for Phil, their interest in the frozen flesh pecked Barrie Jones was fading. Fresh meet in the form of him and his daughters awaited and they were eager for a taste. He turned and ran toward Gaby and Sophie who was visibly distressed, hugging Teddy with tears rolling down her cheeks. Phil, although no slouch, was unfortunately not as quick on his feet as he so desperately would have liked and Sophie's cries quickly turned to screams when three of the faster geese caught him up and began pecking at his legs rabidly.

Phil, trying to both run and kick away the geese, lost his footing and fell heavily to the floor, twisting his left ankle. He scratted frantically, pushing and throwing as many geese as he could but his efforts were futile. There were simply too many and they quickly overpowered him, ripping through his clothes as they brutally pecked away at his body.

"Sophie run, take Gaby and run!" he screamed, now completely surrounded by frenzied feathered geese.

Sophie closed her eyes tightly, buried her head into Teddy and covered her ears with her arms. She was doing everything possible to ignore what was happening. Gaby on the other hand slept through her father's screams and her sister's cries, oblivious to any danger.

The geese were relentless in their attack, quickly stripping the skin and pecking away at the fatty tissue beneath. Phil's death was quick but agonising. Agonising not only for him, but for his daughter Sophie who in spite of her efforts, could not block out her father's screams. Even after his violent death, she could still hear the painful and torturous yells reverberating around her head. Then another high pitched scream penetrated her ears. Gaby was awake and her cries had alerted the once white but now blood stained Geese to their presence. The geese had enjoyed their main and now it was time for dessert but before they could decide which sister they wanted to eat, a tall man with black hair and a long black leather coat appeared, as if from nowhere, wielding an elderly persons wooden walking stick and with it, began to smash and crush the flesh eating birds. The man made short work of the geese, quickly killing them with the stick. He then walked to Gaby who was still crying in her pram and took her in his arms, gently rocking her in the hope she would settle.

"What's your name little one?" the man asked of Sophie.

"My Dad told me never to talk to strangers," a teary eyed Sophie replied.

"Your Dad's a wise man. My name is Nick so now you know who I am and we're not strangers anymore ok?" Nick said softly.

"Ok," Sophie replied. *"My name is Sophie and that's Gaby. Those duckies they... what did they do to my Dad?"*

"Sophie I need you to listen closely. It's not safe on the streets anymore. I need both you and your sister to come with me. I can keep you safe Sophie. Do you see that big building just behind you?" Nick said, pointing to Churchill Mansions, a high rise tower block overlooking Mersey Road, *"That's where I want to take you. I promise it's safe in there and no more bad things will happen ok? Once inside, I will do what I can for your dad."*

Sophie nodded and walked with the man who knew well enough that Phil was dead, he had seen the attack from a balcony on the top floor of Churchill Mansions and had struggled deeply with the decision to help or not.

"Can you take us home? I want my mummy and she is very poorly, like Teddy," Sophie asked showing Nick her teddy bear.

"Let's just get you and your sister inside where it's safe first then we'll talk about your mum," Nick said, knowing very well that *'very poorly'* meant the odds of her still being alive were slim at best.

Sophie followed Nick towards Churchill Mansions and the promise of safety, only stalling briefly to consider looking back towards her fallen father. She would have looked too, if it wasn't for Teddy, who didn't think it a good idea.

Journal Entry 5

Full of adrenalin *(it's the best painkiller)* and with battle paddle in hand, I was ready to go. The staff room of the Grange Comprehensive School was no longer a safe haven after being compromised in an incident that cost Mr Kelly his life and we had no choice but to get out of there. Now it was time to leave the school but my legs were not having any of it. The pain from my back injury meant I was now moving slower and more gingerly than the zombies that were occupying the playground.

"Hey Mr Diant, I reckon you could pass for a zombie with your pale complexion and the way you are walking. Maybe if you walked out into the playground first, the zombies would think you are one of them and you will go unnoticed?" Jonathon said, standing in the doorway of the main entrance looking out to the playground of the dead.

"Because you're handy with a cricket bat and saved my daughter's life, I'm going to let that one slide but you only have a limited number of free passes kid, so use them wisely smart arse, or you'll be getting a crack around the head with this paddle. Got it?" I replied.

If I'm honest, he was starting to grow on me but I wasn't about to let him know that. When it's the end of the world, you have to take your fun were you can get it. Besides, I was still struggling to get my head around my daughter having a boyfriend. Oh, and the skinny jeans. No man or boy should ever be seen wearing skinny jeans. Apocalypse or not, skinny jeans are never a good look.

There was sense in Jonathon's comments though. Ridiculous as his idea was, the truth was we needed a plan to get past the zombies in the playground and through the gates to 80s Dave who was hopefully safe in his Ford Thunderbird. From our position just inside the main entrance, it was impossible to tell what lay beyond the gates. The playground was scattered with meandering zombies and there was a large gathering pressed up against the gates, trying to get to what was on the other side. Something beyond the gate had their attention and I was hoping it was Dave. The only way to find out was for Emily, Louise, Jonathon and I to figure a way out of Hell's Playground.

"Can somebody think of something please, before we all like get totally eaten to death?" Louise said, cowering behind Emily.

Part of the school playground doubled up as a staff car park and in it was a silver Vauxhall Corsa.

"It's a pity none of us can drive," I said.

"Emily can," Jonathon interjected, which was met with a stern look from my daughter that said *'Shut the fuck up!'*

"Dad, I can explain..." Emily started before I cut her off.

147

"Emily, I'm not angry. Given the current situation we find ourselves in I'm prepared to let it go, for now. But just answer me this. Who taught you how to drive? It was your Uncle Butty wasn't it?" I said to Emily who replied by nodding sheepishly.

"I knew it! That god damn survivalist nut job! I'll kill him when I see him," I raved.

"To be fair Dad, the reason Uncle Butty taught me how to drive was because there might be a zombie apocalypse," Emily replied.

I've lost count of the amount of times Butty has started a sentence by saying "In the event of a zombie apocalypse...."

"In the event of a zombie apocalypse, there's a crossbow under your bed."

"In the event of a zombie apocalypse, I've started a vegetable garden on the roof. The dead will contaminate the ground and I am not eating a carrot grown in soil where a zombie has drooled."

"In the event of a zombie apocalypse, I've been storing tins of spam since 1986."

I could go on but I'll spare you, for now.

Anyway, I could forgive my fifteen year old daughter knowing how to drive. Zombies, boyfriends, driving - I was

148

just glad she was alive. Old world problems suddenly seem less important when faced with death at every turn.

"The Corsa over there belonged to Mr Kelly. As he has no use for it anymore being dead and all, one of us could go back to the staff room and grab his keys? If we could make it to the car I could drive it through the gates," Emily suggested.

Well she was right. Simply walking across the Devil's Playground and climbing over the gates wasn't an option. Sure we could probably get past the scattering of zombies that were mindlessly wandering around but the large gathering at the gate? That would be too much for the four of us to handle. Well, three, no, two and a half. Louise was shaking like a shitting dog and my back injury meant most of the work would be left to Emily and Jonathon. Mr Kelly's car was the only option.

"I'll go," Jonathon offered.

"Be careful," Emily said, kissing him passionately for good luck *(an awkward moment for yours truly I can tell you!).*

"Don't start clearing a pathway to the car without me. It's too dangerous and you'll need my help. I'll be back before you know it," Jonathon said before running off to the staff room.

Well, my mind was shot I don't mind telling you. Day one of the zombie apocalypse and my daughter and her

149

boyfriend were acting like they had been ready for this day their whole lives. Was it violent video games, TV and movies that were responsible for desensitising the youth of today? Or in my daughter's case, my brother! Maybe with youth on their side they were just fearless. I felt like I could take on the world when I was her age but zombies? Emily's life up to this point had not been without its ups and downs. Never having the chance to bond with her mother must have influenced her upbringing deeply. The only adults she has ever had to look up to have been me and Butty. Now I love my brother dearly, but he is not the best role model for children. For Emily's first birthday he bought her a Swiss Army knife and a first aid kit. Mental I tell you. Or he would have been twenty four hours a go before this town went to shit. Now he seems the sanest person alive!

"Are you ready to kill some zombies Dad?" Emily said, readying her hockey stick for action.

"So, you and Jonathon ...?" I asked, thinking it best to throw the question out there and get the awkwardness out of the way sooner rather than later.

"Eight months. I'm sorry I never told you about him. It's awkward you know? You still see me as your little girl and I didn't want you to freak out. He's really nice and funny too. You two should spend some time together and get to know each other when we get to Uncle Butty's." Emily replied.

"I wish you would have told me about him sooner and that it didn't take the apocalypse for me to find out you have a boyfriend. But I understand why and I'm sorry you felt you couldn't. The truth is, you'll always be my little girl, even if the past few hours have taught me that you're more than capable of taking care of yourself. I know, I know, your Uncle Butty taught you. I won't know whether to kill or hug him when we get to his place." I said.

"Don't worry Dad, I won't keep anything from you again, I promise. Now let's kill some zombies," Emily smiled.

"I'll just stay back here whilst you do the killing if it's all the same with you," Louise said, still cowering behind my daughter.

"Don't worry Louise, we'll be out of here before you know it," Emily said, placing her arm around her friend to comfort her.

"Got them, you guys ready to move?" Jonathon said, returning with the car keys.

I looked out to Hell's Playground. There must have been fifteen or so zombies bumbling around aimlessly. Beyond the playground at the school gates obstructing our path to freedom, was roughly another twenty zombies, their hands reaching through the gates trying to get to what was on the other side *(hopefully Dave)*. Mr Kelly's car was directly in front of us, 40ft away. Easy you say? Not with my dodgy back and with a bunch of flesh hungry teenagers

151

ready to guzzle you up. Thankfully, they had yet to acknowledge our presence. Instead they just stumbled around, stopping occasionally and groaning. Typical teenagers.

"It's hard to tell if they are dead or alive," I said, offering a smirk to Emily who dismissed my poor attempt at a joke with a *'tut'.*

"Because all teenagers do is wander around sulking? Ha-ha good one Mr Diant," Jonathon said.

"Kiss ass," I replied. *"We need to move slowly and quietly. Any noise is likely to alert the zombies to our presence. We should move in single file and take out the zombies only if they approach. I'll go first."*

"Ok Dad, but there is no way you're leading, your back isn't up to it. It'll be me, Jonathon then you and Louise. We stand a better chance that way." Emily said.

Once again my daughter was right. There was no chance I could lead, not with the pain I was in.

"How many of those kids do you know?" I asked my daughter, looking out to the Devil's playground.

"None of them," she replied, looking at her zombie school mates. *"I mean, I used to know them. You see that girl over there, the one with her jaw missing? Well that used to be Lisa Allen. She sat next to me in Geography class. And do you see that boy crawling across the ground over there,*

the one with his left foot missing? That used to be Zak Smith, Lisa's boyfriend. They had been together since junior school but look at them now Dad. They don't even know each other exist anymore. Over there, by Mr Kelly's car, that used to be Jade Dawber and do you see the dismembered arm she is chewing on? That belonged to Kristina Hunter. I recognise the friendship band on the wrist. No doubt the rest of her will be around here somewhere, unless that's all that remains. You see Dad, I knew who they used to be, but now, I don't know them at all. All I know is, they got ill, they died and then they came back. Now they want to eat us; every single one of us. But they've never met the Diant family before have they Dad?"

"I've got to limit the amount of time you spend with your Uncle Butty," I smiled and kissed my daughter lovingly on her forehead.

"Are you ready? Let's go..."

Town Hall of the Dead

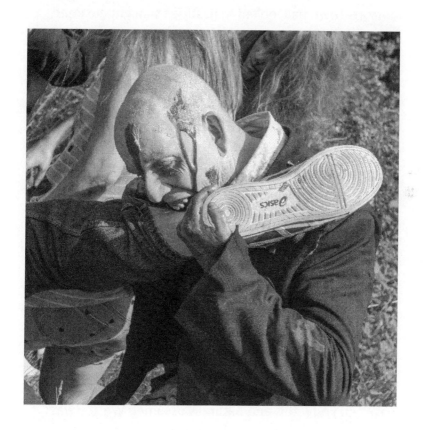

Wesley stood waiting outside the wrought iron gates of Runcorn Town Hall, gazing at the frost coated grass in front of him. It was a cold and crisp winter afternoon. Runcorn Town hall looked majestic as sunlight gleamed down onto its Tuscan style porch. It was a beautiful building; built in the mid-1800s, it was styled to replicate an Italian villa and painted in brilliant white. Once home to Runcorn's wealthy, it now belonged to Halton Council and, in 1964, an office block was built to the rear of the town hall, which housed council employees. Halton Grange, as the picturesque mansion was originally named, was now mostly used as a wedding venue, for those preferring a civil ceremony to a church wedding for their special day.

A golf ball trundled into Wesley's line of sight, closely followed by a small boy not more than eight years of age but Wesley didn't notice. His thoughts lay elsewhere. The boy was carrying a nine iron golf club, too big for his small frame but he was enjoying practicing his golf skills none the less. He looked over at Wesley who continued with his thoughtful stare ahead, the boy invisible to him. The boy wasn't to know this and naturally assumed Wesley was gawking at him and thought it best to go on the defensive.

"Like what you see paedo?"' the boy shouted.

Wesley quickly snapped out of his daydream, noticing the boy then realising that his innocent musing may have been construed as a deviants advances. He dropped his stare and moved towards the Town Hall gates sheepishly, not

155

wanting to draw attention to what was nothing more than an innocent misunderstanding.

"Yeah jog on you fucking nonce, I'll have the police on ya!" the small boy shouted, waving his golf club in the air triumphantly.

Wesley risked a glance at the wedding guests that had gathered. He was safe. None of the thirteen guests that had turned up appeared to have noticed his little altercation with the boy. He played with his neckerchief in an attempt to loosen the restriction around his neck, a bead of sweat dripping from his forehead as his fingers pulled the silk material away from his skin. He hated dressing up and would rather be married in jeans and a t-shirt than be fully suited and booted. But it was what Heather wanted and Wesley wanted nothing more than to give his beautiful wife to be the perfect wedding day.

The nervous groom looked at his watch. It was 12:35pm, and he was due to be married at 1pm.

"Where the hell is everyone?" he said to himself.

He began to wonder if choosing to have his wedding on a weekday to save money had been such a good idea. Surely if invited guests couldn't get time off work they would have told him right? He was starting to have doubts and his concern grew. Not for himself but for the future Mrs Wesley Jones. He wasn't to know however, that Heather Colquhoun had her own problems to contend with.

Heather was at the home she shared with Wesley, where she had been all morning, struggling to be ready for the greatest day of her life. They lived in a 3 bedroom semi-detached house on Cherry Tree Avenue, which was on Runcorn's Grangeway Housing Estate. The estate primarily consisted of ex council houses and bungalows for the retired. Heather had argued that the house was too big for them but Wesley insisted. He'd always been a planner and had one eye on starting a family in the not too distant future. This house was perfect with its large front and back gardens and spacious living areas. What's more, as an ex council house it was an absolute steal and they simply had to have it. Wesley can be persistent and after some intense begging and pleading, he got his wish and the house was theirs. They had never looked back.

Heather had planned the morning of her wedding meticulously. The hairdresser was to arrive at 9am and the make-up girl at 10am, then the wedding car at 12.30pm to take both her and her Maid of Honour Beki to the Town Hall. None of which had happened. Heather had spent the morning frantically trying to call everyone that had let her down but without success. When the phone line wasn't engaged, it was ringing out, and her mobile phone had lost its signal altogether. It was the same for Beki, who had taken on the roles of make-up artist and hairdresser for Heather and herself. Heather was frantic with worry, concerned that she wouldn't be ready for her own wedding. She couldn't believe that everyone had let her down. How could this happen? Beki was riddled with guilt as it was on her recommendation that Heather had hired the make-up girl and hairdresser. They had been absolutely brilliant for her when she tied the knot to become Mrs Rebecca Fairhurst; of course she would recommend their services to her best friend.

Gareth felt like a spare part as he sat quietly on Wesley and Heather's couch, his Cannon 500id camera hanging uselessly around his neck. Normally, he would be using this time to take photographs of the Bride to be getting ready. Angry and crying brides are not the most photogenic so he thought it best to keep a low profile. Instead he was spending his time offering to make cups of tea and helping out where he could, which included offering to take Heather and Beki to the Town Hall, if they were ever to be ready on time. But until then, he would sit quietly and drink his tea whilst he tried to send a text to his friend and colleague Simon.

"Hi mate, not 2 gd here. No makeup, hairdresser or car. Bride in bits. Not sure guna b on time. Try n stall. Thnx."

Send.

Your message could not be sent at this time. Please try again.

158

He tried several times to text Simon but every message came back with the same error.

"I'm just going outside to see if I can get a signal," he said to the girls. *"If I can, I'll get word to the Town Hall and let them know what's happening."*

"Thanks Gareth," Beki responded, Heather being too upset to talk. *"But don't go too far will you? We're relying on you getting us there."*

Gareth left Wesley and Heather's house walking onto Cherry Tree Avenue, all the time looking at his phone. Still no signal, not even a bar. He continued to walk along the street until he felt his right foot sink into something soft and squidgy. He grimaced, assuming he had stepped into dog faeces. He looked to the ground and what he saw made animal excrement a preferred alternative. His shoe had come down heavy on a dead bird, a pigeon to be exact. His heel had pressed into the pigeon's breast, separating its chest cavity, spewing out blood and innards onto the pavement.

"Great, just great," he said whilst wiping the bottom of his shoe on the side of the pavement.

He looked up and noticed that in the road lay another dead pigeon and ahead of that a dead black bird, then further on from that was another pigeon.

"What the hell is going on?" he said to himself, lifting his camera to his face to photograph the feathered bloodbath.

It was then he heard a car screeching in the distance, the noise of its engine getting louder by the second. He watched as the car came into view, hurtling down Grangeway Road towards his location, swaying widely from one side of the road to the other. Whoever the driver was, looked to be completely out of control.

Gareth noted that the car was a Mark 2 yellow Ford Escort, the very first car he had ever bought. He loved that car and memories of driving it came flooding back. Two memories in particular came to mind. He remembered that when driving at night he had to decide between using the lights or listening to the radio as the Mark 2 couldn't handle both and that the guy he sold it to later locked himself in his garage, turned on the Mark 2's engine and with the fumes, killed himself.

"Joy riders," he said, annoyed at the complete lack of respect these kids were showing his favourite car of all time.

He watched as the Mark 2 narrowly missed collisions with the many parked cars on Grangeway. Gareth could make out at least two passengers sat in the back seats of the car, with the front passenger seat being empty. The driver, although hard to tell because of the distance, looked young, possibly late teens but more importantly, whoever they were, appeared to be asleep.

He began waving his arms, shouting frantically in an attempt to get the driver's attention but the car continued on its unruly journey. He could only watch as the car mounted the curb, crashed through a brick wall then ploughed into the side of the Parish of St Andrews Church. The driver, not wearing his seatbelt was projected through the windscreen, hitting the church wall head first, his body lying in a heap of blood and broken bones on the car bonnet.

Gareth felt guilty that his first concern lay with the car and not the people in it. Putting thoughts of his first love to one side, he sprinted to the church, the seriousness of the crash becoming clearer the closer he got. On arrival, it was obvious to him that the driver was dead. His mangled body lying bloodied made that evident. His attention moved to the two passengers that remained in the vehicle but the rear car doors had become jammed and he could not open them. Using his elbow, he broke through the rear door window of the Mark 2 and peered through the broken window. Inside were two teenagers, a boy and a girl, both no more than sixteen years of age. The girl was unconscious, head bloodied and slumped forward against the back of the driver's seat. The boy's left leg had slid underneath the front passenger seat and was only visible from the knee.

"*Are you ok, are you hurt?*" Gareth said to the boy.

"*Is he dead, my brother?*" said the boy, motioning to the pile of mangled bones resting on the bonnet of the Mark 2.

He could see the sadness in the boy's face. The boy already knew the answer but he needed confirmation.

"*Yes, he is,*" Gareth replied softly.

The boy closed his eyes and started to breath heavily, in through his nose and then out through his mouth, as if forcing himself to park this tragic news somewhere deep within his mind so he could focus on himself and the girl next to him.

"*My leg's stuck, I can't move, please help my girlfriend, I don't think she's breathing,*" the boy replied.

Gareth placed his arm through the broken window and tried to open the door from inside. His hand fiddled with the inner door handle but it wouldn't budge.

"*Don't worry mate, I'll get you out of here as soon as I can,*" he said to the boy, attempting to calm his nerves.

He forced his upper torso as far into the broken window as he could. Shards of jagged glass still attached, ripped through his shirt, shredding skin from his chest to his stomach. Gareth gritted his teeth to hide his pain; the boy was looking pale and shivering. Shock had taken hold and he didn't want to make the situation worse for him. He stretched as far as he could and with his fingertips, pulled on the inner handle of the front passenger door. It opened and he breathed a sigh of relief. Finally he had a way to enter the car. Now all he had to do was dislodge himself from the broken passenger window and the glass that was piercing his skin.

Gareth closed his eyes, held his breath and with all his strength, pushed himself backwards out of the car window. The pain brought on by glass slicing through his chest and stomach felt like nothing he had experienced before nor did he want to again. He lurched forward and opened the front passenger door of what was once his favourite car of all time but after it had just carved his stomach and chest, he was reconsidering his choice.

"Hey kid" he said to the boy who was fading rapidly, *"What's your name? Can you hear me?"*

"My name, my name is David, David Goodall. Please, help my girlfriend. She needs help, she needs…" the boy slipped into unconsciousness.

Gareth took one more look at his phone but still no signal. He couldn't risk waiting any longer and had to get the kid out of there. He yanked the front passenger car seat forward which freed the boy's leg. He reached into the back seat and pulled the unconscious David towards him, removing him from the car and laying him on the gravel walkway outside of the church.

"Hey David, can you hear me? Come on stay with me, David!" he said, whilst gently slapping the boy's face attempting to wake him up.

David did not respond. Gareth positioned his ear close to the kid's nose and mouth, listening for any breathing but there was nothing. He commenced CPR, fearing the worst.

Behind him, on the bonnet of the Mark 2, the mangled body of the driver began to twitch. The brother of David placed his right hand on the bonnet and then his left, pushing down with his arms to lift up his torso. He then turned his head to face Gareth, sniffing the air intently. The left side of the drivers face was severely damaged with the majority of his lip missing and the flesh that once covered his cheek bone now hanging by a small thread of skin.

Gareth continued to administer chest compressions to David, counting them to thirty then giving two rescue breathes, all the while unaware of what was transpiring behind him.

David's brother used his arms to drag his body from the bonne, falling heavily on the ground. Gareth, on hearing the noise, turned to see what had caused it.

"What the fuck?" he exclaimed.

Gareth looked upon David's brother, his bloodied gums and teeth visible where his lips used to be and gore filled gloops of drool projected from his damaged mouth. His flesh torn cheek revealed the thin buccinator muscle underneath. David's brother dragged his body along the gravel towards Gareth using only his arms. His contorted, limp and lifeless legs now useless.

Gareth walked towards him, hypnotized by what he was seeing. How was he alive? What was he trying to do? Questions hurtled through his mind as he tried to make sense of what was happening.

David's brother was now within touching distance of Gareth's feet, his bruised and bloodied hands reaching out wildly at the photographer's shoes. Gareth had already subjected one of his shoes to squashing through a dead pigeon; he didn't take to the idea of dirtying them further. He took a step backward and pressed up against something that stopped him from retreating further. He turned to see the cold, pale face of the boy he had tried to save.

"David, you're..."

This was to be his final words as David leapt forward, sinking his teeth into the neck of the man who helped him. Gareth reached out for something to push his attacker away. What he grabbed was the arm of David's brother who rapped his gore torn hand around his wrist, pulling himself forward. The carcass that was David's brother was now close enough to feast upon his succulent flesh. The lipless mouth of the hungry zombie sunk into Gareth's lower arm, ripping the flexor muscle clean from his wrist.

……………….

Wesley's best man Jamie, was leaning against the Town Hall gates, bent forward, vomiting into a bush. Heather had voiced her doubts to Wesley concerning his questionable choice for best man. Jamie Simpson was not the most reliable of her future husband's friends and Heather held him in low regard, referring to him often as a *'bad apple'* and one whose primary concern was for himself. Jamie would agree, shameless in his selfishness. He had made it clear from the moment Wesley asked him to be best man that he was only doing it *'for the birds'*, his eye firmly set on Heather's chief bridesmaid Beki. Beki being married only made the chase more exciting. In fact he preferred it that way as one night stands were a hobby of his and married women meant the chance of any kind of commitment was slim. Beki wasn't the be all and end all for Jamie though, as anyone would do after a couple of drinks.

"This is a disaster," Wesley said to Jamie, who was busy spitting out acidy globules of bile.

Wesley incorrectly assumed that the cause of Jamie's vomiting was heavy partying the night before. You can forgive him for being mistaken as Jamie was blaming this also. Something much more sinister was at work within his body that nobody could have foreseen.

Jamie reached inside his jacket and pulled out a hipflask, drinking from it greedily as if the whiskey inside held the cure for the evil that ailed him.

"Want a swig?" he said, offering his hipflask to Wesley.

"I'd rather drink my own urine filtered through your sweaty socks than put that hipflask anywhere near my mouth. Are you sure you're alright? You've been throwing up for 20 minutes," Wesley replied, remembering Heather's concerns about his choice for best man and thinking she may have been right.

"I'll be fine mate, don't worry about me. I just need to shake off this hangover and I'll be good to go," he responded then quickly returned to throwing up in the bush.

Click!

Jamie lifted his sweat soaked head to see what had made the clicking noise, a trickle of puke dripping from his chin.

"Smile for the camera," said Simon, as the lens from his Cannon 50d intruded Jamie's personal space.

Simon was one half of the of the Wedding photography duo Simon & Garth's Uncle. Garth's uncle, or Gareth as he was more commonly known, was to be arriving with Heather and her Bridesmaid, or so Simon thought.

Simon Martindale lived for photography and loved working weddings. He would take enormous pleasure in capturing all of the special moments that would last forever in the images he created. However, this was one wedding he had not been looking forward to. Not because of Wesley and Heather; both Simon and Gareth thought that they were lovely and they had thoroughly enjoyed photographing the couple's engagement shoot. It was for reasons more personal to him as his ex-wife was a guest and no doubt, her new fiancé would be accompanying her. He had thought it quite mean of Gareth to not swap duties with him so that he could be with Heather and Beki and not have to photograph the guests as they arrived. Little did he know of the unfortunate end to his friend's life that was happening not five minutes away from his location.

Simon had been married once before he met his current fiancé and love of his life. He often commented on how unfortunate he was to have had to go through a divorce before he finally met the woman he was destined to be with. His marriage, to put it plainly, was a mistake and he would be the first to tell you. They were both too young and neither had any idea what they wanted from life. It didn't take long for them to realise that what they actually wanted wasn't each other and the marriage ended within its first year. It became apparent to him that they had absolutely nothing in common. He had many interests such as photography, cycling and playing Rugby, where as it appeared to him the only thing that interested Lucy was her. How he didn't see it from the start was still something that baffled him. Lucy was and still is one of the most self-centred people he has ever known. Everything she says and does is for her own personal gain. No act of kindness comes without its repercussions.

Lucy Howes had also recently become engaged. Simon did not love Lucy anymore, in fact the only feeling he held for her currently was disdain. What made this difficult was her new partner, Anthony Rosenberg, was also a wedding photographer. She had shown no interest in Simon's business whilst they were together but since her relationship with Anthony, she had gone out of her way to make sure her future husband was more successful than her last. Simon had never met Anthony face to face, but he knew who he was and he was aware of the underhand tactics he and Lucy had used to take business away from him and Gareth, undercutting them by more than 50%. But as he had often said *"You get what you pay for"* which with Anthony and Lucy, was a cowboy service and awful wedding photographs. Simon & Garth's Uncle prided themselves on the quality of their work and although business had suffered due to Anthony and Lucy's sneaky schemes, they knew it wouldn't take long for word to spread of their terrible service and business would once again pick up. It was just a matter of time.

Simon heard the all too familiar irritating high pitched squeak that was his ex-wife's voice, coming from the Town Hall car park.

"Come along Anthony, we're late enough as it is, we haven't got time for you to be ill. What on earth will people think of me when they see you looking all ghastly? Suck it up man for God's sake." Lucy squawked, walking away from Anthony who was slowly walking behind her, handkerchief covering his mouth as he attempted to keep his vomiting at bay.

The first thing he noticed about Lucy was how beautiful she still was. She had always taken great care of herself and the years had treated her well. Any old feelings that seeing her may have rekindled were soon buried though. Hearing her squeaky overpowering voice was enough to see to that.

"Wesley my dear!" Lucy bellowed as she rushed over to the increasingly worried groom.

Lucy and Heather were work colleagues. Not one to miss an opportunity to parade her self-importance in front of strangers, she had pestered Heather until she had no choice but to include her as a wedding guest. Wesley had only met Lucy once, at Heather's work Christmas party. She had spent the whole night trying to persuade him to hire Anthony as their wedding photographer. Within the first two minutes he had decided he disliked her. Wesley hated arrogance and snobbish behaviour, the two things that Lucy excelled in. He hadn't told her but he had known Gareth for many years and hiring Simon & Garth's Uncle to photograph his and Heather's special day was never a doubt.

"Sorry we're late Wesley darling but Anthony here has had a dicky tummy. Honestly, you'd think he was dying the way he's been carrying on. No sign of Heather yet?" she squeaked.

"No nothing yet, she will be here any minute now. We should be inside really but the council are late opening the Town Hall doors," he responded.

"I wouldn't worry too much sweet heart. I am sure she will be here soon enough. It takes some people longer to look beautiful than it does others," she said whilst pouting at her reflection in her make-up compact.

For the first time in a long while, Lucy noticed something other than herself whilst gazing at her reflection. Behind the image of herself in the mirror, in the distance, she noticed her ex-husband, taking pictures of the few guests that had gathered. She turned to watch him work and it struck her instantly how professional he was compared to her cowboy fiancé. She didn't linger on this for long though; craftsmanship was never something she had concerned herself with. She just wanted to win and more importantly, to run Simon & Garth's Uncle out of business.

Not that Gareth had ever done anything to warrant being professionally ruined by her. He was just a casualty of war as far as she was concerned.

Anthony could not recall ever feeling so sick and he was sick a lot. If he sneezed, it was flu, if he had a sore throat, it was tonsillitis, if he had indigestion, it was a heart attack. He was a classic hypochondriac and Lucy could be forgiven for not taking his ailments seriously but today, he really was sick and he could feel his body failing. He slumped up against the Town Hall gates close to where Jamie was wilting. He held his handkerchief over his mouth as a way to prevent his vomiting. It wasn't an effective method and brown puke stains were clearly visible through the thin white cotton. He felt completely empty and hollow inside. Where was this vomit coming from? A question Jamie had also been asking himself.

"Fancy a swig?" Jamie said, wiping puke away from his mouth with the sleeve of his rented suit jacket, offering Anthony a sip from his hipflask.

"What's in it?" Anthony enquired, his face scrunched up in response to how repulsive Jamie appeared.

Jamie had been sweating so profusely his once light grey suit had turned black in colour. He sniffed his hipflask.

"I don't know actually. It smells like whisky but tastes like vodka. Vhosky?" he replied to Anthony, who was starting to wish he'd chosen someplace else to slump up against.

Anthony shook his head to the offer and swiftly threw up in to his handkerchief, chunks of puke spraying out either side of the cotton tissue.

Jamie shrugged his shoulders. *"Suit yourself. You look like shit by the way,"* he said, and then gulped again from his hipflask before returning to vomiting in the bush.

Lucy looked over to Anthony in disgust. How dare he be ill and ruin her day. How he behaved reflected on her and she wished she'd left him at home. She looked again to Simon but decided against talking to him. If only Anthony wasn't making such a show of her then maybe she would have conversed with her ex-husband, revelling in gloating about how busy their photography business was. But now that Anthony was playing up it had put her on the back foot and she wasn't about to let Simon have the upper hand.

Anthony felt his stomach churn, only this time it wasn't the precursor to vomiting. His bowels needed to evacuate their content immediately and he had little time before he was to soil himself. He ran up the steps to the Town Hall doors and tugged on the door handle but it was locked. He looked around frantically. What was he to do? Stabbing pains shot from his stomach to his backside and he doubled over in pain. The Chinese Gardens to the rear of the Town Hall - he could go there, but he would need to be fast. He quickly scurried back down the steps and past Jamie who still had his head buried in the surrounding greenery. Anthony frantically wove in and out and around guests that blocked his path to the Chinese Gardens. He turned his head and risked a look to see if Lucy had noticed his awful predicament. Luckily for him, she hadn't and she was too busy looking at herself in her make-up mirror, making sure she looked as perfect as possible. He was safe and made it to the gardens relatively unnoticed. Apart from Simon that is, he had been watching and photographing the whole thing.

Simon knew Anthony had run off because he had diarrhoea. He could tell by his frantic butt clenched shuffle that was more than a walk but not quite fast enough to be a run. Anyone who has ever had 'loose bowels' and had to make the sudden and terrifying dash to the lavatory would recognise that walk and as a fan of spicy food and takeaways, he knew it very well.

Simon had an idea, an evil thought hijacking his mind. If he could get a picture of Anthony soiling the Town Hall's gardens then he would never work again. It would be his revenge for the years of Lucy and Anthony steadily ruining his and Gareth's livelihoods. Just one picture could change everything and he need not worry about their underhand tactics again. Would he be sinking to their level? Sure, but what's good for the goose is good for the gander. He reasoned that if he was in Anthony's position, then Lucy and her future husband wouldn't think twice about doing this to him.

Simon waited a few minutes then followed Anthony into the Chinese Gardens, camera ready, poised to take the picture that would restore Simon & Garth's Uncle back to the top of Runcorn's wedding photography tree. Even Simon could not have hoped for the sight that awaited him. He walked into the gardens to find Anthony face down on the ground with his pants around his ankles, spraying brown water all over the beautifully kept garden. Jackpot!

………………..

With minutes to spare before her wedding, Heather was finally ready and all set to leave but where was Gareth? It had been 15 minutes since he left the house trying to obtain a mobile phone signal and he had yet to return.

Heather reached for her phone. Still no signal. This whole day had so far been a disaster and she was starting to think there was a conspiracy at work, plotting to prevent her and Wesley from getting married.

"I just want to get married!" Heather screamed, *"Why is everything working against me?*

Beki Looked to the couch where Gareth had been sitting and noticed his car keys had fallen out of his pocket.

"Gareth's left his car keys. Come on let's go, I'll drive. If we leave now we can make it. I'll write him a note so he knows what's happening should he come back," she said.

Beki scribbled down a rushed note for Gareth, unaware that if he did come back, he would have little interest in reading.

Gareth,

We've taken your car and gone to the Town Hall. We couldn't wait for you any longer!

Heather & Beki.

Heather composed herself, grabbed her bouquet and ran for the front door. Beki had no sooner finished penning her note for Gareth when she heard Heather's screams from the hallway and the front door slamming shut. She ran to her friend to see her stood with her back up against the front door holding her left wrist with her right hand, blood seeping from what looked to Beki like a scratch mark. Behind Heather, hands were visible slapping against the frosted glass of the door.

"What's happened?" she asked, the petrified face of Heather telling her that something was seriously wrong.

"A crazy homeless man tried to grab me as soon as I opened the door. He scratched my arm," Heather shakily replied looking at her wrist as blood dripped onto her wedding dress.

"My dress is ruined," she wept. Her tears quickly turned into anger. *"That fucking dirty fucking homeless twat has ruined my fucking dress! I'm going to kill the fucking fuck!"*

176

she screamed, pushing herself past Beki and rushing to the kitchen where she retrieved a large carving knife.

Heather was seeing red, her mind blinded by rage, she returned to the front door which was now being guarded by her friend.

"Heather calm down, you need to think about what you're doing. It's just a small stain on your dress. I think we could fix it. Don't do something you will regret," Beki pleaded, but her words fell on deaf ears.

The culmination of everything that had gone wrong had created a monster. Heather could think of nothing but revenge and the 'homeless' man on the other side of the door was something that she could use to project all of her hate.

"Move out of the way Beki," she spoke through gritted teeth.

"Heather please just think... "

Beki never had chance to finish her sentence as the hands from the 'homeless' man came smashing through the frosted glass of the front door, his rancid fingers shredding her throat from her neck. Blood sprayed from her torn jugular vein as the man's hands ripped through her flesh, coating Heather's face and dress.

The man forced his head through the broken window pane of the door and started to chew on Beki's shoulder, his skin tearing on the sharp shards of glass that still remained in place. Beki was dead. The only thing holding her up was the man's grip on her throat as he scoffed on her shoulder.

Heather looked down at her once ivory wedding dress and her vision blurred with rage. Without thought, she charged forward and stabbed the man through his left eye with the carving knife. There was a disconcerting 'popping' noise as it pierced through the man's eyeball and continued its journey on a steady incline to the brain. Heather stepped back, leaving the knife hanging from the man's face whose arms loosened from Beki's neck and she slumped to the floor. Heather's mind could not process what had just happened and instead produced only one thought...

"You're getting married."

Beki's corpse lay in an increasing pool of her own blood, the keys to Gareth's car grasped in her hand. Heather prised open Beki's hand and removed the keys. She stepped up to her front door where the dead man's head remained squashed through the broken window pane. She pulled the knife out of his head resulting in congealed blood and gore squelching from the hole where his eye once lived. She opened her front door. The dead zombie remaining lodged by his head, swung with the door as it opened. She ran outside and pressed the key fob on Gareth's car keys and heard the sound of doors unlocking and saw lights flash on a blue Vauxhall Corsa. Heather opened the car door, sat inside and started the engine.

She glanced back at her house and the dead man slumped in the open doorway. Beyond the man she could see the blood covered legs of her dead maid of honour. She looked at the clock on the car dash board. It was 12.57pm. She had three minutes before she was due to be married.

....

Wesley looked out over the park in front of Runcorn town hall, watching the road that ran adjacent to the council grounds, hoping to see his would be wife arriving in her wedding car. Nothing, but he had noted how quiet the road was for this time of day. Heath Road was well used and gave direct access to Runcorn town centre as well as operating as a main route to the other housing estates in the area. He looked again at his watch; it was 12:57pm. Every scenario possible ran through his mind. Had the registry office made an error and got the date of his wedding wrong? Is that why the town hall wasn't opening its doors? Had *he* got the date of his wedding wrong? Had Heather called the whole thing off? What the hell was going on?

He heard a noise behind him and turned to see Anthony pulling on the handle of the Town Hall doors ferociously before running down the steps, barging past the small amount of wedding guests then entering the Chinese Gardens to the side of the Town Hall building. He noted to himself that Anthony moved like he had diarrhoea. He recognised that awkward jittering run all too well. He

179

watched as Anthony moved from sight, followed soon after by his wedding photographer Simon.

He noticed Lucy also, feigning looking at herself in her compact mirror but actually watching Simon follow Anthony. She waited till they were both out of sight then tailed them both.

He looked to the greenery outside of the town hall and to where Jamie had been standing but to Wesley's concern he was no longer there. He looked closely at his surroundings, trying to locate his best man but could not see him anywhere.

"Great, now my best man has done a runner and I've got guests running off into the council gardens to take a shit. Fucking marvellous," he said to himself.

....

Jamie's 'hangover' had been progressively getting worse as the day moved on. His clothes were soaked with sweat and his body began to shake uncontrollably. His vomiting had appeared to have subsided for which he was eternally thankful. He needed something to sort him out as the content of his hipflask *(whatever it may be)* was failing to do the trick. He had stumbled along the path leading away from the Town Hall and reached a small duck pond situated within the council grounds. He slumped himself down on a bench that overlooked the pond, watching ducks struggle to walk over the frozen water. He reached inside his sweat soaked jacket and retrieved a small bag of cocaine and a thin drinking straw. He opened the bag and placed one end of the straw inside and the other up his right nostril. Jamie had heavily abused his left nostril the night before and decided it would probably appreciate a rest. He closed his eyes and with a long hard sniff, snorted the entire content of the bag.

For an instant, he felt alive, the dark heavy cloud that had invaded his brain appeared to have cleared and the aches that had penetrated his body momentarily lifted. He felt the best he had in years, his body tingling from the feeling of cold air on his sweat sodden skin. He rose to his feet and outstretched his arms as he breathed in the cool winter's air. Every sense came alive with his vision transforming from an unclear daze into high definition. The brown and green colours of the ducks feathers that appeared so dull not minutes before now seemed so vivid. They revitalized him and he laughed as he watched the mallards struggle to walk on the thick ice of the pond. Sounds of wind swirling through the trees became so clear he swore he could make out every rustle of every leaf. He truly felt on top of the world. Then suddenly and without warning, just as he thought he was cured of his 'hangover', his world came crashing down.

Something began to burn within Jamie's brain, causing him to collapse to the ground in pain. The fire inside his head expanded quickly, causing pain like never before. he began to scream, both of his hands squeezing his head in an attempt to subdue the wildfire inside. Then nothing - the pain disappeared as quickly as it arrived. He looked again across to the ducks on the pond and noticed something that had not been apparent to him before. The ducks were not only struggling to walk on the ice, but they were fighting to stay alive. He watched as the duck closest to him no longer possessed the energy to rise to its feet. Instead, it lay on the ice, beak open, choking. He watched it died, then the same thing happened to another and another. Just as he tried to make sense of this, the fire returned only this time it was not in his head but in his stomach. He fell forward, one hand holding his waist and his other steadying himself on the ground. He once again began to be sick, producing brown bile and spittle. He felt as if his digestive organs were being driven upwards from his stomach. He looked at the gravelled ground now covered in bile, watching as the colour of his puke changed from a rich brown to a dark red. It was blood, and he was starting to think that his heavy partying had resulted in him paying the ultimate price.

Just as Jamie's vomiting again began to subside, a golf ball rolled into the small puddle of bloodied bile.

"Hey mister, can you pass me my ball please?" said the young boy with the nine iron golf club.

Jamie picked up the blood and sick covered golf ball and offered it to the boy.

"Actually mate, you can keep it, I don't need it anymore," said the boy, as he backed away from Jamie and his spew coated golf ball.

Jamie collapsed on the gravelled ground; his body shaking as one by one, his organs began to fail him. The boy stopped moving away and instead watched on as Jamie's body twitched and jerked at speed for several minutes before finally ceasing. He was dead. The boy had thought as much, as this wasn't the first dead body he had seen that day and it wasn't to be his last. The boy positioned himself in a defensive position and raised his nine iron golf club, ready to strike. He began to count.

"1... 2... 3...4... 5..."

As the boy reached the count of five, Jamie lifted his head from the ground, his complexion a cool light grey, the change apparent in spite of his fake tan. His white sunken eyes fixated on the boy and he began to rise.

The boy, with his nine iron raised, ran at Jamie and with one heavy but accurate swing, brought the golf club into contact with his head, shattering his skull.

"Fucking zombies," said the boy.

....

Simon could not believe his luck. There in front of him lying face down in the grass with his pants around his ankles, shitting for Britain was Anthony. Simon brought his

Cannon 50d camera to his eye and began to snap away, taking photographs of him in his unfortunate predicament. Beyond Anthony, shadowed by hanging tree branches stood a woman, a woman which Simon recognised.

"Melanie? Melanie Evoy?" he shouted.

Melanie was Runcorn Council's registrar and she was scheduled to be marrying Wesley and Heather. Simon had known her for several years as more often than not, she would be marrying the couples that hired Simon and Garth's Uncle as photographers. He considered her a friend.

"Melanie, are you ok? You know you're supposed to be marrying Wesley and Heather in a few minutes? The doors to the building are not even open yet, everyone's catching a death," he said walking towards his friend.

The closer he got the more concerned he grew. Not only did she not answer but she didn't even acknowledge his presence, it was difficult for him to see, but from where he was approaching, she appeared to be holding something and devouring it eagerly.

He pulled the hanging tree branches away to reveal Melanie held in her hands a dead pigeon and her face was buried inside the bird's chest.

"Fuck me!" Simon exclaimed as he watched her rip chunks of the pigeon's innards, slurping it down her throat.

Melanie sniffed the air, taking in Simon's scent then, lifting her head out of the pigeon kebab, she turned to face him. A harrowing sound projected from her mouth as bits of pigeon hung from her teeth.

"What are you doing?" Simon asked, a joint look of panic and bewilderment on his face.

She dropped what remained of the pigeon and advanced towards him, arms grabbing as she inched closer to her would be meal. Simon stood his ground, more through confusion than anything else.

She reached out grabbing his shirt, leaning in with her teeth chattering inches from his face. Simon pushed against her shoulders, preventing her from biting him.

"What the hell are you doing? Melanie stop it, STOP IT!" he yelled, pushing out at her with strength.

The force in his shove sent her tumbling backwards, falling awkwardly and snapping her left ankle.

She began to rise to her feet, her ankle twisting further as she placed weight on the shattered bones. The expression on Simon's face changed from confusion to horror as she once again began to stagger forward, her mouth gnashing, eager to bite down on his flesh.

"Melanie stop, please!" he pleaded but her mind was no longer open to interaction. Instead it now operated on primitive instinct alone and that instinct was to feed.

185

"Melanie please!"

She continued to advance.

"Melanie!"

She edged ever closer, arms outstretched and mouth gnawing, the harrowing sound of the undead exhaling as she chomped at the air in front of him.

"Melanie stop!"

Simon's pleas continued to fall on deaf ears.

He had to act fast. She was now once again inches away from grabbing him. He removed his camera from around his neck and held it in both hands. With a powerful swing he smashed the camera across the head of his undead friend, bringing her crashing to the ground.

Simon collapsed to his knees in despair, his face contorted with remorse as he began to cry for the friend he assumed he had killed.

"Oh God I'm so sorry, I'm sorry Melanie, please forgive me, please forgive me..." he cried.

Melanie's head began to move and her bloodied face turned to him. Her mouth opened wide andn bits of chewed pigeon became visible from the back of her jaws. Simon lifted his camera above his head and repeatedly

186

smashed her over the head till both his friend and his camera were no more.

"Anthony! What the bloody hell do you think you are doing? Pull your trousers for up heaven's sake you're making a show of yourself and more importantly, me!"

Simon recognised that the squawking behind him belonged to his ex-wife. Lucy had followed them into the Chinese Gardens, but had she witnessed what he had done to Melanie? That was the only thought in his mind, until he heard the groans.

"Anthony, what is wrong with you, why are you grunting like that? And going to the toilet in the council gardens, I mean really? Dear God have some decency and dress yourself. I can see you penis!" Lucy complained.

Simon turned from his deceased friend to see Anthony had risen to his feet and was shuffling towards Lucy with his pants around his ankles.

"Anthony get away from me, you smell of poo," she demanded.

Anthony continued trundling towards her.

"Anthony get off you're ruining my dress," she pleaded, *"This is an original Stella McCartney replica and I don't want your grubby hands touching it."*

He grabbed hold of Lucy's dress and pulled her close. With his jaws open, he bit down hard on her cheek, tearing the heavily foundation applied flesh from her face. She screamed, striking her fiancé repeatedly in the chest with her fists but Anthony had a strong grip and wouldn't be letting go. Opening his mouth wide, he ripped the right ear from her head.

"My earring!" she screamed.

Even when faced with being eaten alive she was superficial.

Anthony pulled her to the ground and continued to tear away at her face. His hands entering her jaws; he tore her mouth apart, splitting the philtrum of her top lip to the base of her nose. Blood from her wounds poured into her mouth and she began to choke. He then proceeded to rip Lucy's lips from her face then shovelled them into his mouth. The pain became so intense she passed out whilst her once hen pecked fiancé continued to devour her.

Simon watched on, panic and terror setting in. He needed to get out of there. The one thought his mind could process was to run and run he did, past his dying ex-wife and her fiancé whom, with a face full of face, lashed out at him in an attempt to grab him as he dashed past.

Simon dodged Anthony's reaching arm and exited the Chinese Gardens. If only he wasn't in such a hurry, he would have heard the engine of the Vauxhall Corsa as it ploughed into him.

………………..

Wesley was close to tears. He couldn't believe what a disaster his wedding was turning out to be. His bride hadn't arrived, the town hall was closed, his best man had gone missing and almost all of his guests hadn't turned up. What was he to do? It was now 1pm and he should be inside, marrying his beautiful bride, not stood outside in the cold all alone but for a few guests and a guy he hardly knew who was busy taking a shit in the Chinese Gardens.

Just as he was ready to give up, he saw a Vauxhall Corsa being driven erratically along Heath Road, heading towards the town hall grounds. He thought he recognised the car and as it approached he realised that it belonged to Gareth. His heart filled with hope. Was this Heather?

The Corsa turned into the town hall grounds, not showing any signs of slowing down. Wedding guests screamed as they dove for cover, avoiding being hit by the oncoming vehicle. Simon didn't stand a chance. Blinded by fear he rushed into its path, the force of the impact flinging him high into the air and propelling him backwards almost 10ft.

Wesley watched in horror as Simon's body hit the ground and then rolled a further 5ft before finally resting motionless. He looked again at the car, expecting to see

Gareth driving but instead his blood stained, knife wielding wife to be was behind the wheel, eyes wide and a crazed expression on her face. Heather left the vehicle, knife in hand with her face and wedding dress covered in the blood of her deceased maid of honour.

"Am I late?" she asked Wesley.

"Heather, what the hell?! Your clothes? Your face? What happened to you? You've just ran over our wedding photographer! Where's Beki?" he asked frantically.

"She's dead. Come on we've got to get married," she replied, gesturing for him to walk with her to the town hall.

She took two steps then fell to her knees, holding her stomach.

"Heather are you ok, what's the matter?" he said as he rushed to help her.

He knelt down next to her and noticed the deep scratch on her wrist.

"What's happened to your wrist? Heather talk to me, you're scaring me. Is this your blood?" Wesley continued, concerned with both Heather's mental and physical state.

"No it's Beki's blood," she replied, then vomited heavily, covering Wesley's suit in puke and bile.

"We need to get you to a hospital," he said, helping her to her feet.

"No!" she screamed, placing the blade of her knife to his throat. *"Today is my wedding day no matter what, you WILL marry me. GOT IT?"*

"Got it," he agreed, fearing for his life then she vomited directly into his mouth.

The warm, acidy puke rushed down his throat and he began to choke. Acting on instinct, he pushed against Heather, thrusting her backwards, her body turning as she fell and the knife she was holding entered her chest, killing her instantly.

Wesley had not seen any of this as he was busy coughing and clearing his throat of Heather's throw up. He cleared the last remnants of spittle from his mouth and turned to find the woman he loved lying dead. He rushed to her side, sobbing wildly. He turned her over so she lay on her back, the knife still protruding from her chest. His tears ran freely as he rested his head against her chest, repeatedly sobbing her name. The surrounding wedding guests had split into three factions. Those that had gone to help Simon, those that had moved to help Wesley and Heather and those that had stayed where they were, not knowing what to do.

As Wesley continued to cry into her chest, her hand began to twitch and it shakily rose from her side, slapping down on his arm. Feeling the movement, he lifted his head and held Heather's twitching hand. Hope began to fill his heart.

"Heather?" he asked.

She jaggedly turned her head to face him. The sunken white eyes of the living dead glared at him and she opened her mouth, letting out a screeching noise like nothing he had heard before.

"Heather you're alive!" he cried.

But she wasn't alive, not medically anyway and she grabbed his head, pulling him down towards her mouth and tore the nose from his face. Wesley screamed in agony as blood leaked from the hole in his face. It didn't take long for Heather to chew through the nose cartilage and no sooner had she finished, she pulled him in for another bite, this time ripping skin from his neck.

Wesley yelled in pain and reached for the knife in Heather's chest. With both hands he pulled it free and stabbed her again, desperate to stop her advances. Despite the fresh wound, she continued to maul him. He stabbed her again and again and again, crying heavily as he did so. Heather relentlessly continued to attack, tearing through his shirt and ripping into his waist. He quickly began to fade as she chewed through his torso, plucking him from life.

The guests that had gathered to help were now running away in fear. Those that hadn't would soon wish they had when out of the Chinese Gardens came Anthony, sucking on the chewed off hand of Lucy.

....

Simon woozily opened his eyes. With blurred vision and muffled hearing he looked up at the wedding guests that had rushed to his aid.

"He's awake. Can you hear me? Sir, can you hear me?" a man asked Simon.

"What happened?" Simon asked, his speech slurred.

"You were hit by a car, you're lucky to be alive, you should be dead," the man replied.

The words *"Alive"* and *"Dead"* repeated in Simon's mind over and over and the horror of the moments leading up to his accident came flooding back.

"We've got to get out of here," he said as he struggled to his feet.

"Pease Sir, stay on the ground your hurt. One of the other guests has gone to get help just stay lying down until we can get someone to look at you," the man said.

Simon knew he was right. His body creaked and cried. Every muscle in every limb felt like it had been hit by a train but he had to move and move quickly.

"No you don't understand... " Simon started but was cut off by Wesley's cries as Heather ripped the nose from his face.

"What the fuck?" the man said, mouth open, stunned by what he was witnessing.

"Now, we've got to go now, it's not safe," said Simon.

"What the hell is she doing?" the man asked.

"She's trying to eat him. Please help me up," Simon asked.

The man helped Simon to his feet. *"I've got my car. Come with me, I'll take you to the hospital and we'll get the police,"* he said.

To get to the car, they would have to walk past the entrance to the Chinese gardens and Simon had no intention of leaving in that direction.

"No!" Simon yelled *"It's too dangerous, there are more of them."*

"I'll be fine. You stay here and I'll bring the car around, you're in no position to walk anyway," the man replied as he ran off towards the car park.

Simon was in no state to protest any further. He looked over to Wesley and witnessed him repeatedly stabbing his wife to be, only for her to rip into his waist, tearing the skin from his side. He glanced back towards the man whom, during this entire hellish nightmare, had tried to help him, and saw him run past the town hall towards the car park. As he reached the entrance to the Chinese Gardens and the small crowd of wedding guests, Anthony stumbled out of the gardens, chewing on Lucy's chopped off hand, minus his pants.

He watched as the small crowd of guests screamed and ran away from Anthony but the man who had helped him was not so lucky. He was intent on getting to his car and had not noticed Anthony at first. By the time he did, it was too late as Anthony dropped Lucy's hand, and threw himself on top of his unsuspecting victim, zombie tackling him to the ground while scratching and tearing at the man with his gore stained hands.

Simon couldn't watch anymore. He had killed his friend Melanie, watched Anthony kill his ex-wife, been run over by Heather, watched her eating her would be husband and now the man who had tried to help him was being eaten too. He needed to get away as quickly as he could but he was hurt, badly. Nevertheless, he summoned the strength to stand and began to hobble away from the Town Hall, taking the path that led towards the Grangeway Estate, past the duck pond.

Simon reached the duck pond, the screams behind him becoming fainter with every step. He was really struggling with his injuries now and wasn't sure how much longer he could keep this up. He stopped and rested with his hands on his knees for support and then he smelt it - the rich metallic smell of human blood. He looked to his left to see that lying on the gravel next to the duck pond was Jamie, Wesley's best man. Well he assumed it was Jamie. His head was so damaged it was difficult to say for sure.

He had to keep moving. He had realised that whatever this was, it had to be bigger than just the wedding. He needed to get help. He turned away from Jamie to continue his journey when he spotted his friend and business partner Gareth on the path ahead of him.

"Thank God," Simon said with new found hope.

He summoned the energy to pick up the pace and he hobbled as fast as he could towards his friend. When he got to him, it wasn't the Gareth he had known.

"Not you too?" He cried, exhausted and dejected. He didn't possess the energy to continue and collapsed at the feet of his friend.

Gareth had seen better days. Both of his arms were torn and ripped and hung by his side with little to no use. His stomach was completely shredded with intestines swinging freely. He didn't need the use of his arms for this meal though as Simon had made it easy for him. Gareth simply dropped on top of his friend and with his mouth began to rip at his body.

Simon didn't fight back or even make a noise, for before Gareth had taken his first bite, he had already died.

Behind Gareth, on the ice of the pond, one of the deceased ducks started to twitch.

Journal Entry 6

I quietly opened the door and Emily made the first move, exiting the school and entering the Devil's Playground. She crept up behind the first zombie obstructing our path towards the late Mr Kelly's Vauxhall Corsa and drove her hockey stick into the back of the undead teenager's head. One down.

"Ew Emily! You've just killed Michael Shellshear," Louise squeaked, cowering behind me.

"He was already dead Louise, you can't kill what's already dead. Plus, you hated him anyway, he was always setting your hair on fire in science class," Jonathon said.

"That doesn't mean I wanted to see his head get caved in with a hockey stick," Louise replied.

"Shh please! Keep it down you two!" Emily said with a threatening whisper.

We moved slowly forward. With the first zombie in our path taken out it was now time for the next. Jonathon moved ahead of Emily and with his cricket bat, bashed a small zombie girl over the head.

"Good night Laura Woodcock. You being a zombie? It's just not cricket," Jonathon whispered to the fallen zombie.

"Does he think he's in a movie?" I asked Emily.

198

"Apparently so," my daughter replied quietly. *"Hey, Rambo! No more one liners ok?"*

I remember feeling useless watching Jonathon and my daughter do all the dirty work whilst I slowly limped forward; the pain in my back preventing me from helping as much as I would have liked. Making it worse was Louise cowering behind me, pulling on my jacket with both hands as if it offered some sort of protection.

Emily and Jonathon continued to work together, clearing a path to the car whilst keeping a careful look out for each other. They made quite the team and given the horrific circumstances we found ourselves in, I could not help but feel proud of my daughter, if not a little concerned at how quickly she was adjusting. I was going to have to have words with my brother about this. This was definitely that crazy bastard's influence.

Emily moved forward, another zombie down.

Jonathon moved forward, another zombie down.

As we advanced, I felt the pain in my back begin to ease and my posture improve. At first I thought the slow but fluid movement was helping but then I realised the real reason. Louise was no longer pulling on my jacket. I turned to see her petrified, no longer moving forward but backwards towards the doors of the school.

"Louise, what are you doing?" I hushed.

"I can't, I can't, I can't, I can't, I can't..." Louise cried, not half as quiet as I had hoped her reply would be.

Louise's cries had alerted two zombies that were stumbling close by.

"Louise, quickly, you've got to move now! Please Louise," I begged but my plea was wasted, she was too far gone to hear me.

She gripped her waist tightly and lowered her head; her petrified face hiding behind her long black hair. Whimpering and shaking with fright, she repeatedly said *"No"* whilst shaking her head violently from side to side. I hobbled towards her as quickly as I could. Using the battle paddle, I smashed the first zombie over the back, knocking him to the ground. Using the heel of my boot, I again and again brought it down on the zombie's head until it resembled a fleshy trifle. Now for zombie number two. I swept the legs from under the dead teenager and quickly stabbed the paddle into its forehead.

I would like to tell you that killing zombies was becoming easier but it really wasn't. The sound created when breaking someone's skull or the cold sickly shiver that runs through your body when turning a zombie's brains to mush, are things you never get used to.

"Louise it's ok, just come to me, we'll be out of here soon, trust me," I pleaded.

It was no good. Louise's fear had taken her to a place where there was no coming back. Her continued backward movement had led her into the open doorway of the school and behind her stood the newly deceased Mr Kelly.

"Louise!" I yelled.

Both Emily and Jonathon paused their zombie slaying to see why I was causing such a commotion. Louise turned to face her zombie headmaster who stood, towering over her, saliva dripping from his flesh hungry mouth down onto her poor, petrified face. She screamed, alerting all of the zombies in the playground to our presence. The zombie headmaster chomped hard on Louise's face, ripping her eyeball from its socket. Oh man, I swear I saw her eyeball burst in Mr Kelly's mouth when his teeth bit into it. I definitely heard it pop. Louise was frozen with fear and unable to protect herself as Mr Kelly lunged forward, forcing her to the ground.

"No!" Emily screamed.

"It's too late Emily, there's nothing you can do and we've got other things to worry about," Jonathon said, holding her back.

He was right, they did have other things to worry about. There was now close to twenty zombies closing in on our location. We had to move fast if we were going to make it to the car. Moving I could manage, but moving fast?

Emily, full of anger and pain, lashed out at the approaching zombies, hitting anything that came close with her hockey stick. Louise was motionless, having either passed out from the pain or she was dead. The zombie headmaster had made short work of Louise's face which was now almost completely stripped of skin. Well, I may have been too late to save Louise but I could do something about Mr Kelly. The dead fuck had eaten his last meal.

hobbled forwards. Mr Kelly showed no interest in my presence; instead he shredded away at the fallen Louise, troffing chunks of her into his mouth. Summoning as much strength as I could, I kicked out at the zombie headmaster's head, my boot connecting with his chin. It was a good kick if I do say so myself and the power of it snapped his head backwards and a fleshy tear opened up across his neck. I swung the battle paddle almost separating Mr Kelly's head from his body. Now I've seen some things over the last day and this has to be one of the most disturbing. Mr Kelly's head, having snapped backwards was now flapping like a heavily oiled hinge whilst his teeth chomped together over and over again. I couldn't leave it at that now could I? A few more smashes with the battle paddle ensured Mr Kelly's brain was destroyed and he had chewed on his last human.

Now Louise was dead but how long would she stay that way? I barely knew the girl but she was a good friend to my daughter and I felt I owed it to her to make sure she stayed dead and didn't rise to roam the streets looking to devour the living like the rest of the undead bastards that were rapidly filling my town. I turned the battle paddle around and using the handle end, I smashed it through Louise's forehead, penetrating her brain. I turned and hobbled to join Emily and Jonathon who had done a brilliant job in clearing a path to the car.

I lay in the back seat of the Vauxhall Corsa, the double seat providing some much needed relief for my back. Jonathon sat in the front with Emily in the driver's seat, resting her head against the wheel. Not a word was spoken. All you could hear was the groans of zombies as they started to surround the vehicle, slapping their putrid hands against the cars frame. I decided to break the silence. Not on purpose mind you but by an unwelcome accident. The kind of accident that smells so bad you need to open a window, only opening a window in our case, could mean death.

'Parf' came the noise from my bottom, rudely interrupting the silence.

I tried to seep it out quietly but my arse demanded to be heard.

"Oh Dad that stinks!" Emily moaned, wafting the air in front of her nose.

"It's not that bad," I replied. *"I've smelt a lot worse than that today I can tell you."*

Jonathon began to cough, *"Oh God, I can taste it. It's got right to the back of my throat. I wish I could open a window."*

"Don't you dare open a window, you'll have us all killed," Emily said.

"Death by zombies or your Dad's farts, it's all the same to me," Jonathon replied as he gagged on the stench. *"Mr Diant what have you been eating?"*

"Mayonnaise, the Devil's condiment. As you can tell, it doesn't agree with me," I replied.

'Parf' said my bottom, obviously feeling left out of the conversation.

"My eyes are stinging," Jonathon cried.

"Emily let's get going. If we stay static any longer we will be surrounded by zombies and we'll have trouble moving at all, and put the air conditioning on. I can't guarantee I won't do it again." I said.

Emily put the Corsa into reverse, slamming the zombie school kids that had gathered to the rear. Then she revved the engine.

"Fasten your seatbelts, this could be painful," Emily instructed, before putting her foot down hard on the accelerator and speeding forward towards the zombies clambering at the school gates.

I decided it would be best to sit up for this, heed my daughter's words and strap myself in. My back had improved slightly and I wanted to limit any potential damage.

If anything, the impact wasn't as bad as I had expected. The herd of zombies at the gate had cushioned the blow and the car made it through with very little damage. The problem now was the zombies once trapped in the playground were spilling out onto Latham Avenue. On the plus side, the Ford Thunderbird was still on the road and judging by the amount of undead that surrounded the vehicle, someone was inside.

"That's Dave's car, he has to be inside," I said.

"There is no way we can get to him Dad, there are too many zombies. They're everywhere." said Emily.

"I've had an idea. Mr Diant, how's your back holding up, can you move?" Jonathon asked.

"I'm fine, what's your plan?" I asked.

I wasn't fine, far from it, but I didn't want to sacrifice anymore man points to a kid wearing skinny jeans.

"Follow my lead. Emily, keep the car moving," said Jonathon.

Jonathon lowered the window in the front passenger door, unbuckled his seatbelt and with cricket bat in hand, lifted his upper body out of the vehicle. Emily started the car.

"Come on you dead bastards!" he yelled, bashing anything over the head that came close enough.

"Your boyfriend's got a screw loose you know that don't you?" I said to Emily.

Now it was my turn to lift myself out of the car window and join in with the zombie bashing. Battle paddle in hand, I gritted my teeth and strained my upper body out of the window and a noise left my mouth like nothing I had ever made before. It was a cross between a yelp and a squeak. Luckily only my daughter heard me. Jonathon was far too busy swinging his cricket bat. Man points still intact!

One by one the zombies slowly fell. It wasn't an easy task, far from it, but with my daughter's driving and Jonathon and I swinging like lunatics, we cleared the area of the undead. Well, if I'm honest, it was mostly Jonathon that did all the hard work. I was just hoping he wasn't keeping a kill score. All the stretching had actually done my back the world of good but I was exhausted. Jonathon on the other hand had youth on his side and looked like he could go on forever. All that remained for us to do now was to clear the zombies that surrounded the Thunderbird. There were three left in total and the three of us exited the vehicle.

"Dave must be in there, why else would they be ignoring us?" I said.

"I'm going to enjoy this," Emily said, staring ahead at the zombies slapping their putrid palms against the Thunderbird. *"You see the girl on the bonnet, pressing her hands against the windscreen? That's Beth Roberts and the others are Hannah Oldfield and Emily Bridge, Beth's groupies."*

"The Queen bitches of the school," Jonathon added.

"These girls made Louise's life a complete misery, just because she dressed differently," Emily said. *"Well now it's payback. This is for you Louise."*

Emily marched forward towards Beth and smashed the hockey stick across the back of her head which split on impact, spraying blood and head tissue across the windscreen of the car.

"That was for all of the times you called Louise a Goth, a witch and a freak," Emily cried.

Hannah was next to meet the wrath of my daughter *(never piss off a Diant, especially if you're a zombie)*. She grabbed zombie Hannah by her hair, pulling her away from the vehicle. As Hannah opened her quickly rotting mouth, letting out a harrowing groan, Emily inserted the handle of her hockey stick, forcing it through her putrid throat and out of the back of her head.

207

"That was for the time you set fire to Louise's hair in science class," she cried.

Emily pushed her right foot into the chest of the zombie and slid the hockey stick free from its mouth. Next up was the undead Emily who, during the destruction of her flesh eating friends, had moved her attention away from the car and to my daughter, shuffling slowly towards her.

"I'll take this," Jonathan insisted, running at zombie Emily, smashing his cricket bat across the side of her face.

Teeth, drool and blood flew through the air as the force from the hit sent the zombie teenager to the ground.

"This is for Louise and for the time you stole her diary and read it out in front of everyone. Oh, and for sharing my girlfriends name," Jonathon said before again smashing her in the head with his cricket bat.

Emily was visibly shaken. Losing her friend had hurt her deeply and although killing the zombie girls had relieved some anger, it was going to take more than cracking a few skulls for my daughter's grief to subside. I took her in my arms and held her tightly. I could have stayed like that for hours. For a moment, Emily was once again my little girl and not the capable, level headed young adult she had proven herself to be over the past few hours. For the briefest of moments, she was a child, seeking comfort in her father's arms.

"Guys, I reckon there's someone in here but I can't tell for sure. It's too smokey," Jonathon said, his face pressed up against the driver's window.

Emily and I joined Jonathon at the car. Inside the Thunderbird, it was completely full of smoke and a strong smell of cigarettes seeped through the frame. I pulled on the door handle. Locked.

"Dave!" I shouted, banging on the roof of the car.

Nothing. The three of us shook the car as hard as we could.

"Dave!" I again shouted.

Through the thick cigarette smoke a hand appeared at the window and flicked us the middle finger. We all looked at each other then began to bang heavily on the car whilst screaming "Dave!" over and over again.

Finally the front passenger door opened and 80s Dave appeared in a cloud of smoke.

"Fuck me lar watch the body work it's a classic this car, you're going to ruin it," Dave moaned.

"Christ Dave, are you deaf? We've been shouting and banging on the car for ages," I said.

"I've had me headphones on Ace. Billy Idol lar, you can't whack it. The moaning and groaning from those dead pricks was doing my head in. Looks like you did a good job of shutting them up though. Nice to see my paddle has been put to good use. Good work kidda. I knew you'd make it back in one piece. Is this your daughter then?" Dave said, lighting a cigarette.

"Emily, I'd like you to meet Dave" I said, introducing her to my retro friend.

"Alright girl, nice to meet you. You've got a good Dad here you know? A bit squeamish and not the sharpest tool in the box but he'll do," Dave said.

"Nice back handed compliment there Dave, thanks very much," I said.

"My name is Jonathon, nice to meet you Mr Dave," my daughter's boyfriend interjected, extending his arm for a handshake that wasn't forthcoming.

"What's the deal with skinny jeans over here?" Dave asked, eyeing Jonathon up and down whilst completely ignoring the handshake request.

"He's Emily's er, boyfriend. He's ok Dave. If it wasn't for him, Emily could be dead, me too for that matter," I said.

"Well if John says you're ok then that's good enough for me but the first chance we get, we're getting you a normal pair of jeans. There's no room for skinny jeans in the apocalypse lar," Dave said, sucking down on his cigarette.

"Dad we best get moving. Zombie alert." Emily said, nodding towards the approaching herd of undead shuffling our way.

They were slowly closing in from every direction. We hadn't exactly been quiet and the noise we made waking Dave from his Billy Idol wonderland was like ringing a loud dinner bell for the nearby walking dead.

"Everyone in the car," I said, limping my way to the front passenger seat of the Thunderbird.

"What's up Ace?" Dave asked, *"Why are you walking like you've shit yourself?"*

"I put my back out earlier," I replied.

"Put your back out? Fuck me John you're 34 not 64. Suck it up kidda and stop being a little Princess," Dave replied, showing his usual level of support.

We climbed into the car and instantly began to cough horribly, the stench of cigarettes and lingering smoke quietly coating our throats. Dave was fine though and he looked puzzled as to what the fuss was about.

"Man it stinks in here," Jonathon complained.

"Stop your whinging skinny jeans," Dave said whilst lighting another cigarette. *"It smells a lot sweeter in here than it does outside with all those zombies rotting up our streets. Where too Johnny boy?"*

211

"Weston Road, to my brother's house," I informed.

"Weston Road it is. Strap yourselves in boys and girl, this could get interesting," Dave said, revving the engine of the Thunderbird.

'Parf.'

"Oh Dad!"

Tatts for the Memories

Nick Fieldsend sat on an old rickety wicker chair inside his grandmother's flat, facing an open doorway and looking out to the hallway outside. In his left hand he clutched a freshly opened bottle of Jack Daniels and in his right hand, a blood stained wooden walking stick. It had been several hours since Nick had used the same walking stick to kill his beloved grandmother. Well, she was trying to eat him.

To his right, behind the closed door of his grandmother's bedroom, a softly sung lullaby could be heard. Nick did not recognise the song but he found the soft tones of Sophie singing to her baby sister Gaby comforting.

Close to two hours had passed since he heard the dying screams of the girl's father as he was savagely eaten alive by a gaggle of zombie geese. Close to two hours since he wrestled with the decision to help the girls or not. Helping others had not been part of the plan formulated following his grandmother's transformation from a kind hearted, beautiful old lady to a maniacal, flesh hungry monster. His plan was to secure Churchill Mansions one floor at a time, starting from top to bottom. Once the high rise block of flats was zombie free, he was to board up all entrances and exits. Once this was done, the building and its content would be his. Nick had surmised that when secure, he could live quite comfortably using the bounty of food and drink gathered from the many apartments within the building. What he hadn't counted on was witnessing the horrible death of the girl's father. Knowing they would be

214

next, he couldn't let them suffer the same fate. He had to do something and do something he did.

Now he had a young girl and a baby to care for but for the moment that had to wait. He had to clear the building and his plan to do this was simple. Sit patiently and wait for the zombies to come to him.

Nick took a long drink of Jack Daniels. Sure it was close to 10am but it was the end of days. Time was irrelevant now and if he was going to kill every infected resident in the building, he wanted to be buzzed. As the warm bourbon slid down his throat, he heard a shuffling out in the hallway. Something was approaching and Nick was ready.

For Fran, Katie and Kris, it had been a strange morning at LA Tattoo. Fran had been waiting on a full day sitting that was now almost an hour late and looking like a no show. It was rare for a customer to cancel their appointment with Francis Curran. Widely regarded as one of the best tattooists in the area, it wouldn't be uncommon for LA Tattoo to have a waiting list spanning three months or more for his services.

Kris Evans was ready to throw the shop's laptop out of the window such was his frustration at being unable to establish an internet connection. He had tried everything. System reboots, router reboots, disconnecting then reconnecting cables but nothing had worked. What was

215

more frustrating was his mobile phone also had no internet connection, denying him any access to LA Tattoo's Facebook page.

"Fran, Katie, check your phone, can you get on Facebook?" Kris called from the shop reception to the tattoo studio.

"No," came Fran and Katie's simultaneous response.

Unbeknown to Kris, neither Fran nor Katie had checked their phones. Katie Hayden's attention belonged to a half sleeve skull motif design she was drawing for a customer and Fran was reading his Kindle. Should they have done so, their answer would nevertheless have been the same.

The frustration within Kris was close to boiling point. It was 10am, the shop was empty and due to the lack of internet, he had not been able to get anything done. It was time for a breakfast run.

"I'm going out for food, do you two want anything?" Kris asked, poking his head through the door to the studio.

"No thanks," Katie replied still engrossed in her design work.

"Are you going to Greggs? Get us a couple of sausage rolls, it's hungry work being a tattooist," Fran replied, lifting his head out of his Kindle.

"Hungry work? All you've done is read your book since you came in. What are you reading anyway?" asked Kris.

"It's a horror, proper sick, twisted shit. It's about a bloke who kills people then has a wank over a clock. Alarm clocks, carriage clocks, Grandfather clocks... You name a clock and this bloke has wanked over it. It's really good. You can read it after me if you want to?" Fran replied.

"I think I'll pass Fran, but thanks for the offer. Won't be long." Kris said, grabbing his coat then exiting the shop.

Kris walked out on to Regent Street and it struck him instantly how quiet it was. Although not an overly busy area, Regent Street was home to a sandwich bar, several second hand shops, a takeaway, a florist and a pet shop amongst others. This was strange for 10am on a Monday morning but nothing about that morning was making much sense to him. Maybe paying his regular visit to the girls at Greggs the Bakers would restore some normality. Kris was on good terms with all of the workers in Runcorn Old Town. Being a small shopping area, many of the businesses looked out for and supported each other. He particularly had a good relationship with the girls from Greggs due to Fran's love of sausage rolls.

Kris turned onto Church Street, all the while tapping away on his phone trying to get access the internet. He was so preoccupied he didn't notice the woman lying in the doorway of Aladdin's Pizza, being eaten by two small children and he didn't notice the pet shop and the zombie stood in the window, devouring a rabbit.

Church Street was the main shopping area in Runcorn Old Town but it had gradually depleted over recent years. This was partly due to the Runcorn housing development of the 1970s which created the 'New Town' area and the indoor Halton Lea Shopping Centre, formally named Runcorn Shopping City, and more recently, the rising shop rents and the building of the new Trident Retail Park situated next to Halton Lea. All of this had almost destroyed Runcorn's original town centre which now consisted of mostly greeting card shops and take away joints.

Lifting his head from his phone, he observed how deserted Church Street appeared. Several abandoned cars littered the street whilst every shop was closed including Gregg's and all he could think of was how pissed Fran was going to be when he didn't return with his sausage rolls.

Kris wasn't alone on the street. Beyond the first of the abandoned cars, banging on the window of Greggs were two women and he thought it best if he approached them to see if he could find out what was going on. Crossing the street, a speeding red Ford Fiesta almost took his life when it screamed passed, missing him by an inch before turning onto Regent Street.

"Katie I'm bored," Fran complained, throwing his Kindle down hard on the empty leather tattooing chair, *"That*

chair should have someone sat in it. If I don't tattoo someone soon I'm going to explode."

"Why don't you carry on reading your book? What were you telling Kris, it's about a bloke that shags clocks or something?" Katie replied.

"He doesn't shag them, he just masturbates over them. You make it sound pornographic. Anyway, I had to stop reading because it was making me horny," Fran responded.

"You have some serious problems Francis Curran, you know that don't you?" said Katie, lifting her head from her design work to look at him disapprovingly.

"You sound like my wife and like I always tell her, it's what makes me so likeable. Come on Katie, stop what you're doing and let me tattoo you, it'll help pass the time," he replied.

BANG!

Fran and Katie turned to face the doorway leading to the reception area.

"It's open," Fran shouted.

BANG!

"I said it's open!" Fran shouted again, louder this time.

BANG!

"Fuck me are they deaf or something?" Fran cursed, rising from the comfort of his seat and entering the reception area to answer the shop door.

He was greeted by the sight of two young children. He recognised them as Anthony and Emma Fogg. The children's mother, Julie, owned the flower shop across the road. Anthony was chewing on a decapitated finger and his sister Emma, with her once long and beautiful hair now matted and knotted, dripping in blood. In her left hand was a gore stained teddy bear. In her right hand, she held the dismembered head of her mother and was using it to bang against the shop door.

"Fucking hell that's awesome! Katie come and have a look at what these kids have done," Fran said with amazement, believing what he was witnessing to be an elaborate prank.

"Jesus Christ Fran! You could have warned me before I walked in!" Katie screamed, *"It looks so real."*

"I know it's ace! Well done kids, great job," Fran proclaimed, clapping his hands in approval.

Just then, the owner of the nearby pet store, Thom Martin, appeared at the window of LA Tattoo, ripping into the carcass of a rabbit and shovelling it into his mouth greedily.

"Shit!" Fran shouted, taken by surprise at his appearance, *"Now that is good. That is very good. Am I missing something? Is there some kind of horror carnival going on in the Old Town that I don't know about?"*

"Fran I think that's real" Katie added, moving closer to the window for a better look.

"Get fucked that's not real, it can't be?" he replied, joining Katie for a closer inspection.

Fran looked beyond Thom, to the doorway of the shop opposite LA tattoo. In the doorway stood the owner, Keith Daniel Jones. The right side of his face was missing flesh from the jaw line to lower neck, revealing a thick layer of fatty tissue and blood vessels. Keith had fixed his gaze on Fran and slowly stumbled forward into the road. Had Keith been alive, he would have noticed the speeding red Ford Fiesta before it ploughed into him, launching his body forward through the air, landing in a heap 10ft along the road.

The man in the red Ford Fiesta turned his head towards Fran and Katie and screamed *"Lock the door!"* Then he revved the engine and drove over the twisted body of Keith, squashing his head with the front and then back left wheels before speeding away.

"Where the fuck are the keys?" Fran asked Katie.

"Kris has them," she replied but not before swallowing the bile that had gathered in her mouth.

"How did I know you were going to say that?" he replied.

The closer Kris came to the women the more familiar they were. He recognised the pair as Grace Smith and Jane Goldsmith, both employees of Greggs. Fran had been sending him on breakfast runs to Greggs to get his sausage rolls for so long he was on first name terms with all the of staff but why were they banging on the window and what was wrong with their faces? Looking at their pale, gaunt features he assumed they had both been drinking heavily the night before and turned up for work late and still intoxicated.

"Morning girls, heavy night on the town last night was it? So what's up then? Won't Hannah let you in till you have sobered up? Get a few sausage rolls down your neck, that'll sort you out, just make sure you leave a few for Fran," he said.

Upon hearing his voice, they moved their attention from the window and turned to face him, giving a full view of their grey skin, dark sunken eyes and saliva dripping mouths.

"Holy shit, no wonder Hannah wouldn't let you in. How much did you have to drink last night?" Kris asked.

The girls didn't respond but began stumbling towards him, mouths open and teeth exposed.

"Hey come on now girls, calm it down. I know I'm good looking but you're being a bit forward, control yourselves," he said, trying to politely spurn what he falsely assumed were the girls drunken advances.

Inside Greggs, the shop manager Hannah Bradshaw appeared at the window, her right hand applying pressure to an open wound on her neck and her face filled with fear and drained of colour. Hannah looked at Kris and mouthed the word...

"Run!"

Then she projectile vomited over the window, covering the sausage rolls, pasties and sticky buns that were on display.

"Fucking gross!" he grimaced trying to stop his own spew from leaving his mouth.

Why had Hannah told him to run and how was he going to explain to Fran why he didn't have his sausage rolls were two of the three thoughts circulating around his mind. The other and more important thought was what the hell was he going to do with the approaching Grace and Jane? 'Nothing' was his conclusion and he thought it best to return to LA Tattoo as quickly as possible.

Turned from the 'intoxicated' pair, he looked across the road to the other bakery on Church Street, the Devonshire

Bakery and in particular, one of its employees Ashley Stewart, who was stood behind the counter, throwing meat pies, pasties, breads and whatever else he could get his hands on at a would be attacker that was trying to grab him from the customer side of the counter.

Kris purposefully crossed the street with the intention of helping Ashley and screamed at the attacker to leave him alone. The attacker responded to his yell by turning to face him and Kris realised who it was. It was Ashley's work colleague Lewis Williams and he was behaving exactly the same as the girls. His yell had distracted Lewis just enough to give Ashley time to grab a bread knife and dive over the counter, driving it through Lewis' head, killing him instantly.

Kris felt his entire body spasm as he watched Ashley's attack. From his position he had a perfect view and shivered at the sight of the bread knife poking out of the back of Lewis' head.

"*Run!*" Ashley shouted, then through the door behind him staggered another of his colleagues, Leanne Done.

Like Lewis, Leanne's face was drained of colour with spittle dripping from her mouth. Ashley placed his foot on Lewis's chest and pulled the knife free from his head.

"*Run!*" Ashley again shouted then he dove over the counter, repeatedly stabbing Leanne in the head with the bread knife.

Kris looked behind him to see that both Grace and Jane were within touching distance and beyond them more were approaching. He looked ahead and the scene was worse than behind him. There were over 30 crazed people stumbling his way.

He couldn't make sense of what he was seeing. What had happened to these people? Why were they turning violent? And what of Ashley in the Devonshire Bakery and Hannah in Greggs? The only thing he knew for sure was he was quickly becoming surrounded and he needed to move, and move fast. The only way out that appeared to be lunatic free was Kings Street, situated to his right a little up the road. Kings Street would take him past Churchill Mansions and down onto Mersey Road and the embankment which overlooked the Manchester Ship Canal and River Mersey. It would mean a detour but at least it would take him out of harm's way.

The zombies continued to hungrily gnash their teeth, pressing their quickly decaying hands up against the door and window of LA Tattoo. Fran and Katie had been working hard to secure the shop, piling tables and chairs up against the door and window, just in case one of the undead figured out how to turn a door handle.

"Now what do we do?" Katie asked.

"Back door's locked, we've secured the front as much as we can without the keys, the only thing we can do now is wait and hope that help arrives, or at least someone who can tell us what the fuck is going on," Fran replied.

CRASH!

There was a loud clattering noise coming from the tattoo studio above. The studio upstairs was run by Shaun Wainwright and neither Fran nor Katie believed him to be in work that day.

"Shaun?" Fran shouted.

The response came by way of another clattering sound.

"That sounded like the tattooing chair being knocked over. Did you see Shaun come in this morning? I didn't." Katie asked of Fran who shook his head in response, not taking his eyes from the ceiling.

"Follow me," he said to Katie, who followed him back into the studio.

On the wall hung two decorative Samurai swords. Fran removed them and handed one to Katie. Removing the swords from their sheaths a cloud of dust expelled into the air, filling Fran's mouth and nose, causing him to cough repeatedly.

They were both examining the rusted blunt blades when they heard a harrowing groan and heavy footsteps on the

226

stairway leading from the studio upstairs to where they were situated.

"Whoever it is, I mean Shaun or whoever, if they look like those gross fuckers outside, stab the bastard!" Fran said to Katie who nervously nodded in agreement.

Kris had made it to Kings Street without any altercations. Whatever had happened to these people, coordination and speed were no longer a part of their skill set.

Directly in front of him stood Churchill Mansions, a high rise block of flats that towered over Runcorn Old Town and the River Mersey. To the side of Churchill Mansions lay the path to Mersey Road. He surmised that he could use this route to navigate his way back to LA Tattoo and hopefully avoid any crazies.

Walking next to Churchill Mansions, he felt a gust of wind followed by a loud and disgusting squelching. He suddenly felt wet from the waist down. Directly to his left, not 5ft away, a dead man lay splattered on the ground.

"Sorry about that, but you should really watch where you're walking"

Kris took a few steps backwards and looked up. From a balcony on the top floor of Churchill Mansions a man dressed in black clutching a half empty bottle of Jack

Daniels could be seen peering down at him. It was Nick Fieldsend.

"Hello there! How's it going? Lovely day isn't it," Nick shouted down.

"Are you fucking crazy? What are you doing?" Kris Yelled.

"Just a second..." Nick replied before disappearing from the balcony.

Kris looked at his clothes. From the waist down he was covered in blood and ooze.

THWARP!

Another Body hit the ground, again close to where Kris was standing, missing him by inches.

"Watch out!" Nick shouted.

"You were supposed to say that before you threw the guy from the balcony you crazy bastard!" Kris screamed in anger.

"Oh yeah, ha ha!" Nick replied, taking a large chug on his bottle of Jack Daniels.

"That first guy, his name was Dave Noonan, he lived in the flat next to my Nan's. She lent him her humidifier and he never gave it her back. Got it back now though haven't I you dead shit! The other guy, well that's Jay Parker, he lived along the hall, the noisy bastard. Always playing

crappy dance music, drove my Nan insane. Bootcha, bootcha, bootcha... All fucking night and day! Not anymore!" Nick shouted, taking another swig of Jack Daniels.

"My name is Nick by the way, nice to meet you. Oh and look out below!" Nick continued before throwing another body from the balcony.

Kris heeded the warning and leapt out of the way as the dead woman's body hurtled to the ground.

"What the fuck are you doing man? Why are you killing these people, what's wrong with you?" Kris screamed.

"They were already dead. They all are," Nick replied, pointing to the hoard slowly shuffling towards Kris from Church Street.

"What are you talking about? How the hell can they be dead?" Kris asked.

"You see that woman splattered on the ground next to you? Her name was Nicola Mercer. Now she was actually a really nice lady, until she died, came back and tried to eat me. Good job I had a walking stick handy and smashed her skull before she had chance to chow down," Nick said.

"You're not making any sense," Kris cried, exasperated.

"Everyone is dead. You see those people stumbling towards you? Dead - all of them. It's the end of the world my friend.

People have been getting sick, dying then coming back to eat your BRAINS! I'm talking zombies fella! The undead, walkers, shufflers, deaders or whatever you want to call them. Hang on a second..." Nick said, disappearing from the balcony.

Kris looked at the dead that surrounded him, then towards Church Street and the gathering hoard that slowly approached. Even when faced with the living dead, all Kris could think of was how angry Fran was going to be when he returned without his sausage rolls.

"Hey! What's your name?" Nick shouted down, returning to the balcony.

"It's Kris," came the reply.

"Nice to meet you Kris. I've got a gift for you, something to help you on your way. Hang on a second..." said Nick, again disappearing from the balcony.

Could it be true? Was the lunatic right? Was the recently dead coming back to life?

"Going down!" Nick shouted as he hurled another body over the balcony.

Kris watched as the fattest man he had ever seen fall through the sky, plunging towards him. He quickly jumped out of the way and was narrowly missed as the male zombie landed face down on the pavement next to him. Again he found his lower body sprayed with blood. The large bloated bulk of the man Nick threw from the balcony had exploded on impact like a human water balloon, showering him in warm guts. He angrily looked up to Nick who was smiling back at him. He didn't see the point in complaining anymore and instead just shook his head at Nick whose response was to give him a thumbs up.

"There's a present in there for you somewhere. You might have to turn him over though," Nick said, taking another swig of Jack Daniels.

Kris approached the splattered remains of the dead man and kicked him over onto his back, only not all of him moved. What remained of the man's upper torso was embedded into the ground and turning him over, opened him up like a cellar door.

"Ew nasty!" Nick shouted. *"There's a walking stick tucked into his trousers. I'd grab it quickly if I were you,"* he added, pointing to the nearing zombies.

Kris could see the walking stick peeking out from the top of the man's trousers.

"If it makes it easier for you, you know, sticking your hands in a strange man's pants and all, his name is Alex Smith and he was livelier dead than he was living," laughed Nick.

Kris reached for and freed the walking stick from Alex Smith's trousers, albeit with some difficulty. The impact when Alex's heavy frame hit the ground had pushed the walking stick into his flesh and the two had become one. Kris not only had to free the walking stick from the dead man's trousers but rip it out of his thick fat laden leg.

"Can you not just let me in?" he asked of Nick.

"No can do I'm afraid. I've already secured all entrances and exits to the building. It's just me and however many more of these dead fuckers are left inside. As soon as I've destroyed the last of them and thrown them over the balcony, there will only be me left and the building and all of its content will be mine!" Nick proclaimed, lying through his teeth.

Kris wasn't to know, of course, that he had yet to secure the building and with Sophie and baby Gaby now sleeping in his grandmother's bedroom, he was anything but alone.

Nick, hearing a noise from within the flat, once again disappeared from the balcony.

Walking stick firmly gripped with both hands, Kris was gearing himself up to dispose of his first zombies, Grace and Jane, as they stumbled towards him. Just as he was readying himself to strike...

"Look out below!" Nick bellowed as he launched yet another zombie over the edge.

Kris took several steps backwards, having estimating that the falling zombie would crush him if he failed to move. He watched as a headless old lady fell from the sky. Grace and

Jane, both being dead, lacked the function of reckoning and paid no attention to the falling dead woman. If they had then maybe they would have moved out of the way also but instead they stumbled into the increasing shadow of the falling pensioner, which landed on top of Jane, crushing her instantly.

"Heads up!" Nick yelled.

Kris looked up to the balcony to see Nick holding in his hands the dismembered head of the old lady. Letting go of the head, it hurtled downwards landing directly on top of Grace, splitting her skull and killing her promptly.

"That was Gina Noble, an old lady from down the hall. The bitch hated everyone and everything so taking a couple of zombies out with her dead body is probably what she would have wanted. Look, it's been nice talking to you an' all but I'm afraid I've got to leave you to it. I've got a lot of heads to bash before the tower block is mine. Good luck Kris, and just remember one thing and you will be fine. If it shuffles, smash it's fucking brains in! Oh yeah, and if you're heading where I think you're heading, watch out for the wildlife!" Nick shouted, waving goodbye then once more disappeared from the balcony.

Kris, with the other zombies quickly approaching, quickly left Churchill Mansions, heading down to Mersey Road.

The footsteps on the stairway grew closer and the groans louder. Fran and Katie stood waiting, samurai swords in hand, ready to defend themselves from whom or what was approaching.

The first thing they saw was a boot as it hit the top step heavily. Then the second boot followed and gradually their colleague Shaun Wainwright was revealed, one hand clutching his stomach and the other holding his sweat sodden head.

"I don't feel too good," he whimpered.

"Christ Shaun you scared the shit out of us, I nearly stabbed you then," Fran said, relaxing his nervous grip on the sword.

"Stab me? What are you talking about, what's going on?" Shaun asked, bent over with pain.

"Walk through to the front of the shop and have a look, everything has gone to shit." Katie said.

Shaun slowly and painfully walked through the doorway, out of Fran's studio and into the reception area of LA Tattoo. He looked at the furniture piled up and lent forward to peer through a small gap between two chairs. He saw the decapitated head of Julie Fogg being banged against the window then returned to the studio.

"I think I'm going to be si..." Shaun gargled, his mouth filling with vomit before he could finish his sentence.

Fran and Katie dove for cover, Katie under her desk and Fran behind his tattooing chair but their efforts to save themselves from the puke gushing from Shaun's mouth was futile. They were both covered almost instantly and so too was everything else.

After several seconds, Shaun was empty and he collapsed with exhaustion, falling face first into a pool of vomit. Fran and Katie rose to their feet and stood silently, shocked at what had happened. They wiped the bile from their eyes and looked at each other.

"Shaun? Shaun, wake up," Fran said whilst gently rocking his lifeless colleague with his foot.

Nothing. Shaun did not respond.

"Do you think he's dead?" Katie asked, fearing she knew the answer to the question already.

Then a horrendous noise entered their ears as Shaun broke wind, filling the studio with a smell so bad it could curdle custard.

"Judging by the smell I'd say he's still alive," Fran replied, screwing up his face in response to Shaun's stench.

"I've got to get out of this room. My skin is stinging from the puke and I feel I'm getting a nose bleed from the smell," Katie complained as she stepped over Shaun, walking towards the doorway to the reception area.

Shaun's hand reached out and grabbed Katie's left ankle, pulling her to the ground. She turned to face him, her arms holding the door frame separating the studio and reception area. Dripping with bile and saliva, Shaun's face appeared gaunt and hollow. Skin grey with visible dark veins, he chattered his teeth together snapping at the space between Katie's ankle and his face. She tried desperately to wriggle free from his clutches but his grip was strong and using the hold he had on her, he pulled himself up to her leg and bit deep into her ankle.

Katie screamed for Fran to help her and began to kick Shaun repeatedly in the head with her free leg, his face becoming more disfigured and bloodied with every kick. Unfortunately for her, this did little to deter him from chomping on her ankle.

"Fran, help me please! Katie cried.

Fran, who had so far watched in disbelief as events unfolded, ran at Shaun and booted him hard in the side of the face, causing his colleague's jaw to break, freeing Katie's ankle from his putrid mouth. She recoiled into the reception area and Shaun turned to face Fran, rising to his feet with his jaw loose and hanging

"What the fuck is wrong with you?" Fran yelled.

Shaun groaned as he stood upright then let out a petrifying croak from his disfigured mouth. Blood, teeth and spittle flew through the air.

236

Fran now knew that Shaun was one of 'them'. Like the kids and the pet shop owner at the window, he had changed, he was a zombie. He reached for his sword and positioned himself in a defensive stance. Shaun slowly approached and Fran could feel the adrenaline flow through his body.

Then there was the noise. It started as a small rumbling sound that gradually increased in volume, shaking the ground steadily and then the walls. Fran glanced to his tattoo equipment as one by one, inks jittered along his work table, falling to the floor. He looked back to Shaun who was now within touching distance. He raised his sword to strike when suddenly the rumbling became so loud it was unbearable, causing him to drop the weapon and place his hands over his ears. No sooner had his hands touched his head he felt himself propelled backwards and something large and heavy pinned him to the ground. Then silence, no more rumbling. He felt the cold winter's air on his face which was in stark contrast to the warmth that filled his upper body.

He looked up to see sky. The shop ceiling and roof had collapsed and bricks had fallen on top of his lower body, trapping him. From what he could see, very little remained of his studio but the wall separating it from the reception area was still largely intact. Near the doorway to the reception was the large jet engine of a Boeing 737 and poking out from beneath was the crushed hand of his undead colleague.

"Katie?" Fran coughed. *"Katie can you hear me?"*

There was no reply. He tried desperately to free himself from the rubble but his strength was failing. He realised he wasn't going anywhere without help and to make matters worse he had no feeling from the waist down.

"Help! Somebody please help!" he pleaded.

Then a noise; something began to move behind the wall in the reception area.

"Katie! Katie is that you?" he asked.

Through the broken doorway, Katie appeared and like Shaun, she too had turned. Grey of skin and sunken eyed, she clambered over the rubble towards him. He frantically reached out for something, anything he could use as a weapon to defend himself but there was nothing and the reality of impending death washed over him like a cold shower.

She climbed on top of him and opened her mouth ready to eat her first meal as a zombie. With death imminent, all Fran could think of was Kris and how much he really wanted a Greggs sausage roll.

"What the hell happened here?" Kris said to himself as he walked along Mersey Road towards a body almost completely stripped of skin and muscle.

He carried on walking, as further along in the road lay another dead man. Similar in appearance to the first but completely frozen. He felt a knot in his stomach as he looked upon what remained of the man's face. He knew him. Even after having the majority of his features stripped Kris knew him to be Barrie Jones. Barrie was a regular at LA Tattoo and it was he that had missed his slot that morning.

"Fuck me," he grimaced.

With the zombies following him from Church Street, he felt it best to not stay in the same place for too long. He began to move with the intention of continuing along Mersey Road, heading back to Regent Street and LA Tattoo. He hadn't moved more than two steps when he heard the manic quacking coming from the embankment. He turned to see a large gaggle of angry geese with coats of blood stained feathers waddling his way. Now he understood what the crazy bastard at Churchill Mansions meant by *"Watch out for the wildlife"*.

As he turned to run his vision was filled with the sight of an airplane, an Easyjet Boeing 737 heading towards the Runcorn Bridge and where he was situated. No matter how hard he tried, his legs failed to move and he could do nothing but watch as the airplane dropped in altitude and crashed through the bridge arch before continuing to his location. He continued to watch as one of the engines separated from a wing and flew over his head, hurtling towards Runcorn Old Town.

The last thing Kris felt before he died, before the plane crashed into him, was the zombie geese as they surrounded his body and began pecking ferociously at his legs.

The last thing he saw before he died was the pilot of the plane through the cockpit window, being ravenously ripped apart by a zombie stewardess.

Journal Entry 7

Dave drove us away from the zombie massacre at the School. I looked at Emily through the rear view mirror. She looked devastated, having allowed herself a few moments to reflect on recent events. She had not only witnessed her school friends die but for them to coming back and try to eat her. That's more than enough to mess up anyone's head. Then for her to lose Louise the way she did had to have been distressing. I still hadn't told her about Jane. That the car she was travelling in was used to separate the head from her friend's shoulders. Somethings are best left unsaid!

We travelled along Boston Avenue and the park grounds surrounding Runcorn Town Hall. Things had moved on from the mass panic of people leaving their homes and filling their cars with what belongings they had, trying to outrun the apocalypse. Now it was abandoned cars, the dead and living dead that littered our streets.

I looked across to the Town Hall Park and to the path leading to the duck pond. On the path was a zombie on its hands and knees, greedily tucking into the remains of what I thought to be a man, but it was hard to tell as there wasn't much of him left. Behind the greedy dead man stood a zombie bride, covered head to toe in blood. There was no sign of the groom though and something was telling me that the blood that coated her body and dress did not belong to her. I could only imagine the carnage that must have played out. The zombie bride would have awoken that morning expecting to have the best day of her life, not the last.

Dave drove us to the bottom of Boston Avenue and turned left onto Heath Road; a long street with a steady incline. On the left were medium to large sized semi-detached houses. On the right the same but there was also a fire station and, directly ahead, a medical centre.

Dave stopped the car at the bottom of the Road. I want you to close your eyes and imagine what you believe to be a typical post zombie apocalyptic street. Got it? Well that's exactly what Heath Road looked like. Abandoned vehicles in the road. Some on their side, some upside down, some on fire and some already burnt out. One car had ploughed into the front of the first house on the left. The driver, after apparently losing control, had driven the vehicle through the front window of the property. Beyond that on the right hand side of the road was a three car pile-up with several zombies to the side of the crash ripping into the dead body of a passenger that had attempted an escape. Just beyond that was a smouldering transit van and from it crawled the burnt remains of the driver as he tried desperately to join the other hungry zombies ahead of him enjoying their tasty roadside snack.

To the right of the mayhem was Heath Road Medical Centre. With my back still causing me problems, I suggested a quick stop off to loot any medical supplies we might find.

"Dave, we should check out the medical centre up ahead. If it hasn't been looted already they may have painkillers, antibiotics, bandages and anything else we might need. Plus, I could really do with something to ease this pain man, my back is in bits," I said.

"You got it Ace," Dave replied, driving the Thunderbird around the wreckage and pulling into the car park of the medical centre.

The car park was empty but for a Ford Mondeo Estate and the door to the centre was open. This wasn't looking good. The car and the open door suggested any supplies contained inside may have already been looted or even worse; the people doing the looting were still there.

"What do you reckon Kidda? Someone in there?" Dave asked.

"There's only one way to find out," Jonathon interjected, leaving the vehicle with cricket bat in hand, jogging over to the Mondeo Estate.

"A fiver he doesn't make it through the rest of the day," Dave said, offering a small wager on the young lad's life.

"Dave, have you even got a fiver?" I asked.

"No. That's how confident I am that Skinny Jeans over there is going to get himself killed if he carries on like this," Dave stated.

Jonathon had moved away from the Mondeo and was now at the open entrance to Heath Road Medical Centre, motioning for us to join him. Then he walked in! I was quickly coming to the conclusion that this kid was fearless.

"Ready that fiver Ace, it could be pay up time," Dave said, exiting the Thunderbird and grabbing his battle paddle.

Dave, Emily and I reluctantly left the relative safety of the vehicle. Emily had to help me out of the car as my back started to seize up from sitting in the same position for too long. I desperately needed some pain relief.

We cautiously entered the open doorway and like everything else we had encountered that day, it was not a pretty sight. In the patient waiting room stood Jonathon, surveying the bloodshed. Three lay dead sprawled over the waiting room chairs but these were not ordinary dead folk, they were zombie dead folk. Their complexion gave that away.

To the left of the waiting area, behind a desk and Perspex window, slouched against a wall, lay two dead zombie receptionists. Alison Ellis and Lisa Droughton. Well, that's what their name badges said. Their faces were so badly bloodied and disfigured only dental records would identify them. Beyond the waiting room was a small corridor with several doors on either side. One lead to a doctor's surgery, one to a nurse's surgery, two doors for male and female toilets and one door, at the very end of the corridor, marked staff only. This door had been left open slightly, a bloodied hand print smeared across its middle.

Jonathon made a move towards the corridor and the open door only for Dave to grab him by the arm.

"Not so quick Skinny Jeans. As much as I would really like to win a fiver from my good friend John over here, I'd rather have you alive than dead. Don't be so eager all the time Kidda. You never know what or who's waiting around the next corner," Dave whispered to Jonathon who heeded his words, albeit reluctantly.

Together, we walked forward towards the open door. Dave lead the way, followed by Jonathon and then myself and Emily, who was still helping me hobble along, acting as a human walking stick. Dave pushed the door so it opened fully, revealing a man sat on the floor slouched against the wall, facing us, next to a filing cabinet. He was surrounded by opened bottles of pills and blood soaked bandages. The wrist of the man's left arm was heavily bandaged and in his right hand he held a blood stained hammer. The man was unconscious.

"Do you think he's dead Dad?" Emily whispered.

"I'm not sure," I responded, observing the man, *"He could be, he looks pretty beat up."*

"If he is dead, bagsy first dibs on that hammer," Jonathon said excitedly eyeing up the weapon.

"You're dangerous enough as it is, I'm not sure you can be trusted with a hammer as well as cricket bat," I said.

"See those socks over his trainers? Cyclists wear those. Same goes for his leg warmers. What's a cyclist doing driving a car?" Dave asked, lighting a cigarette. *"I'll try and wake him and found out."*

Dave tapped the man on the top of his head with his battle paddle.

"Oi! Lance Armstrong, wake up," Dave said.

The man began to stir and groggily opened his eyes. It took him a few moments to realise where he was and that he wasn't alone. He lifted his hammer clumsily, lacking the strength and co-ordination to hold it with any determination.

"Hey it's ok, we're not going to hurt you. What's your name?" I asked softly, trying to calm the injured man's nerves.

"Rod, my name is Rod Hay," he replied. *"Jesus my arm, I can feel something burning through my arm."*

"Hi Rod, my name is John. This is my friend Dave, my daughter Emily and the kid eyeing up your hammer over there is Jonathon. Can you tell us what happened to you?"

Race for Life

Rod Hay opened the door to his house and exited with his Boardman road bike. Black frame with red trim and handle bars, Rod's bike had taken him on countless adventures. A keen cyclist, he had taken part in many charity bike rides which is why at 7am on a cold Monday morning he was out on the streets, rubbing warmth into his bib shorts and thermolite warmer covered legs, ready to start training for his second coast to coast challenge. The journey would take him the length of England in two days to raise money for Halton Haven Hospice which aims to care for people within the community suffering from life limiting illnesses. He had been fundraising for Halton Haven for several years and he knew that to continue doing this, early morning training sessions would have to become a regular occurrence.

It struck Rod how quite it was for a Monday morning. Being close to the Runcorn Bridge, he expected to hear the roar of heavy traffic as cars and buses transported people to work but there was no sound at all. Runcorn was still and not a twittering bird broke the silence.

He placed earphones into his cold ears, tightened the strap on his cycle helmet and jumped on his bike ready to start his journey when something caught his eye. To his right, on a balcony at the top of Churchill Mansions looking directly at him was a man, dressed in black and drinking from what looked like a whiskey bottle. The man raised his arm and waved at Rod. Not thinking much of it he waved back, pressed play on his mp3 player and started to peddle away.

If Rod had stayed just a few seconds longer he would have watched as the man threw his recently deceased Grandmother over the balcony to the ground below.

The inspirational sounds of the Rocky anthology filled his ears as he headed towards Dukesfield. If there was ever music to get his legs motoring on a cold morning it was the Rocky anthology and it wasn't long before he possessed the Eye of the Tiger. So in the zone was he that when he passed under the arches of the Runcorn Railway Bridge he failed to notice the zombie Lisa Franey as she chomped on the chewed off hand of Dave Gleavey whilst holding the rotting remains of her dead cat Wilf.

He continued on his route, failing to notice the dead corpses floating in the Canal, the man jumping up and down on the head of his zombie wife outside the Railway Public House and the dying starlings on Picow Farm Road. It wasn't until he cycled onto Balfour Street that alarm bells started to ring and he realised that something was very wrong.

After cycling past several abandoned cars, he brought his bike to a halt and turned off his mp3 player, sensing that even having the Eye of the Tiger might not be enough to save him from the chaos in the road ahead. A man lay dead outside the door of the Co-operative Supermarket.

Ripping the dead man's stomach apart was a large older lady, naked apart from the rollers in her hair. Behind them, further up the road, several of the undead crowded around another body only identifiable to Rod as human by its clothes.

Astride his bike, Rod vomited and the loud retching sound that accompanied his heaving was enough to alert the naked lady to his presence. She lifted her hands out of the dead man's stomach and rose to her feet. Blood dripped from her mouth, down through the crevice of her huge swinging breasts and over her hanging stomach. He wiped the trickles of puke from his mouth and watched in horror as the naked zombie waddled towards him. In his panic and eagerness to move, his foot slid from the peddle and he fell to his side. His beloved bike landed on top of him and his foot became stuck between the Boardman's black frame.

He struggled for several minutes to free himself. With panic taking hold, the task took far longer than it should have and as a consequence, Rod's naked older lady admirer was now almost within reaching distance.

He pulled himself together enough to free his foot from his bike just in time to use it as a shield, protecting himself from his wrinkly attacker. He pushed the bike against her dry leather-esque skin and her large drooping breasts bulged through the Boardman's frame like putty dough.

250

She strained her neck, edging her snapping mouth closer to Rod's face.

"Get away from me you crazy bitch!" he shouted, leaning forward and butting her brutally in the middle of her face.

Rod's cycle helmet crashed into the woman's mouth and nose, splitting her top lip and breaking her nasal cavity. This did little to stop her advances and she continued her pursuit, desperate to taste his fresh succulent flesh.

Summing up all of his strength, he ran into the woman as hard as he could, using his bike as a battering ram. Lacking any co-ordination, the old naked lady quickly tripped and fell to the ground landing on her back with the bike on top of her. This was his chance to leave and he quickly headed further up Balfour Street only to be greeted by a one armed heavily tattooed transvestite shuffling towards him. He removed his cycle helmet and taking it in both hands, rammed it hard into the transvestites head, knocking him on his back. The noise alerted the other zombies crowded around the torn apart body and they began to shuffle towards him. To Rod's right was BJ & J Owens newsagents and the graffiti on the window said 'No Zombies.'

"Zombies? Fucking zombies!" Rod yelled.

He looked to the shop door; the sign said 'open'. It was his only option and he hastily entered.

"Dead or alive," Barry asked, holding aloft his axe handle ready to defend himself if need be.

"Alive," Rod replied, his back pressed up against the shop door.

"Right then young man, what can I get you?" Barry said, smiling at his would be customer.

"Get me? Some fucking answers would be nice. What the hell is going on out there? I've just been attacked by a huge naked old lady and a one armed transvestite," Rod asked, his voice breaking with fear.

"Naked old lady you say, hmmm. How big were her breasts?" Barry pondered.

"Massive. They were hanging past her knees." Rod replied.

"Oh that's Julie Holmes, she's alright that one," Barry informed. *"Just as long as she didn't have her teeth in you'd have been fine. As for the transvestite that's Neil Murphy. His other arm is around here somewhere. One of my regulars came in earlier chewing on it."*

"I need answers. That sign, the one on your window?" Rod asked.

Barry proceeded to explain everything that he knew, detailing what had happened to him that morning. From Josh the zombie paperboy, to his regulars that, instead of buying their usual milk and newspaper, wanted to get their hands on something more substantial, and meaty!

"I can't stay here. I've got to get home. My girlfriend Mel, she's at home sleeping, she doesn't know. Wait, shit! She'll be getting up for work soon. I have to leave." Rod panicked, rushing to the shop door.

"I strongly advise you change your mind and stay. You've seen what's out there, it's chaos. This is happening everywhere and it's only the beginning"

"I have to try," Rod replied placing his hand on the door handle ready to exit. *"Thanks for all your help."*

"Here" Barry said, throwing Rod a hammer, *"Take this. You won't get far with just your fists and cycle socks now will you?"*

"Thanks" Rod replied, *"You know you really should lock this door."*

"Lock the door? Nonsense! Apocalypse or not I still have a business to run!" Barry said with a huge smile on his face.

Hammer in hand Rod left BJ & J Owens and walked back out onto Balfour Street. The scene on the street was how he left it. A crowd of zombies continued to pick away at the remains of their victim and he was once again faced with Neil, the one armed transvestite. To the left of Neil was an abandoned Ford Mondeo Estate with the driver door left open.

'Perfect' he thought to himself, only he would have to see to the transvestite shuffler first.

Rod had never hurt anything or anyone in his life but if he wanted to see his girlfriend again, he would have to make up for it. Summoning the will to strike, he screamed loudly and swung the hammer hard into the one armed transvestite's forehead. The blow was enough to put it down for good and he watched as blood trickled from the zombie's open wound, mixing with its perfectly applied mascara.

Looking down at his victim, he felt a dull ache in his left wrist. He lifted his arm to see the sleeve of his cycle jacket was torn and below the tear his skin had been scratched. He looked again to the zombie he had just killed and below the finger nails of his one remaining hand, there was skin. Did the skin belong to Rod? He didn't have time to contemplate this right now as the noise created in killing his first zombie had alerted the hoard picking at the remains of the carcass further up the road.

He was about to make a move for the Mondeo Estate when he heard the scraping sound of something heavy being lugged along the road. He looked down Balfour Street towards the Co-operative supermarket and saw, stumbling forward, the large naked older lady with her right foot stuck between the frame of his beloved Boardman bike. It was a difficult thing for him to see. The bike that had taken him on hundreds of miles of adventures was being savagely mistreated and he wanted nothing more than to take his hammer and bludgeon the old bitch to death. He felt anger swell inside but he had to stay focused. He didn't have time for killing naked old lady zombies, even if they did deserve it.

Instead, he quickly ran to the Mondeo Estate, climbed inside and locked the doors. To his delight the owner of the vehicle had exited in a hurry and left the key in the ignition. He reached to turn the key and start the car when his vision began to blur and he felt sick and disorientated, the interior of the Mondeo spinning and spiralling. He focused his eyes on the gear stick and his vision started to steady, but intense pain penetrated from his arm. He pulled back the sleeve of his cycle jacket to reveal that what only a few moments a go was a small scratch on his wrist had turned into a deeper wound filled with yellow puss and pink ooze. He could feel heat running from the wound and spreading up his arm. He had to get this treated and feared if he did not, he wouldn't make the journey home and more importantly see Mel. His best option was Heath Road Medical Centre, a short car journey from Balfour Street.

With his vision now clear, Rod started the Mondeo Estate and heading towards the medical centre and hopefully, treatment for his wrist.

Journal Entry 7 – Continued

"You're wondering what to do with me aren't you?" Rod said, concerned.

"You've been scratched lar, that means you're infected. Be it five minutes or an hour from now, you're going to become one of them. Judging by the kip of ya it'll be sooner rather than later," Dave replied.

"Maybe we could remove his arm - that might stop the infection from spreading. Rod can we see your wrist?" I asked.

Oh man it was nasty. Clotted blood pulsed up and down inside the deep wound and dark veins protruded from the scratched area, stretching out from his wrist reaching up his arm. This was not looking good for the poor fella. If we were going to remove his arm, we needed to do it quickly and even then, would it really work?

"Nice idea Ace but what are we going to remove his arm with, our teeth?" Dave said.

"Very helpful Dave. Do you know sarcasm doesn't suit you?" I said.

"Yes it does, it's one of my best features. My smile being my best," Dave said, giving the biggest grin you have ever seen, exposing his disgustingly brown, nicotine stained teeth.

"Christ Dave close your mouth, I've seen zombies with better dental hygiene than you," I said.

"Do you two mind, my life is in the balance here!" Rod interjected.

"We could use this," Jonathon piped up, waving a saw around.

"Where the hell did you get that?" I asked.

"I found it. There's a tool box over here next to the filing cabinets. There are all kinds in there, screwdrivers, nails and this saw. They must have been doing some DIY," Jonathon said.

"Well if we're going to do it, it needs to be soon. Look at the veins in his arm lar. The infection is spreading quicker than herpes on a Friday night down the Bank Chambers," Dave said.

For those of you not familiar with the delights of the Bank Chambers, it was a nightclub in Runcorn with a reputation for attracting 'unsavoury' characters. The place had been shut down more than Mega Upload.

"I'll do it," Jonathon eagerly offered, making his way towards Rod, saw in hand.

"Hold your horse's scrappy doo, Rod hasn't agreed to this never mind who will do it," Dave said.

"Do it." Rod said through gritted teeth.

"Are you sure now? There is no guarantee that this will even work; the infection may already have spread," I said.

"If it's the only chance I've got of surviving and seeing Mel again then I want it done but please, do it quickly," Rod replied.

"Well if we're going to do it we should knock him out first. If we don't, the pain will..."

THWACK!

Before I could finish my sentence, Jonathon had taken his cricket bat and whacked Rod over the head. From the impact of the blow, Rod had fallen to his side and blood began to gush from a newly obtained gash on his forehead.

"Oops, bit hard that," Jonathon said.

"A bit fucking hard?" Dave yelled, checking on Rod to see if he still had a pulse. *"You've killed him you daft prick!"*

Dave was right, Rod was dead. Captain ants in his pants had been too eager to help and instead of knocking him out, had accidentally killed him.

"It was an accident. You said knock him out so that's what I tried to do," Jonathon said, his face drained of colour and arms shaking.

"Yes, I said knock him out, not kill him!" I shouted.

"Well I've never knocked anyone out before! How was I to know how hard to hit him?" Jonathon replied, almost in tears.

"It was an accident Dad; it could have been any one of us. Have any of you ever knocked anyone out before?" Emily asked.

"We should go Ace. Grab as many medical supplies as we can and leave," Dave suggested.

"You're right, everyone grab what you can then we're leaving. It's getting dark and it's too risky for us to be out on the streets. Besides, my brother will be waiting. Jonathon, I know it was an accident and you didn't mean for him to die but from now on you don't do anything without running it past me first. Without you, both my daughter and I would probably be dead, I understand that. But if you continue to keep rushing in the way you do, it'll be you getting us killed," I said to Jonathon who stood motionless, focused on the cricket bat in his hands.

Emily comforted him. I know what he did was an accident. Jonathon's a good kid but really, what was he thinking? No, scrap that last bit. He wasn't thinking. He heard me say *"... knock him out..."* then attempted to do just that, only very BADLY!

We were too busy scrounging around for medical supplies to notice that Rod was no longer dead dead, but dead undead, and was greedily eyeing up the human pick n' mix before him. It was Emily who first noticed Rod of the Dead had risen to his feet and was about to wrap his arms around the traumatised statuesque like Jonathon. She was the first to react too, screaming her boyfriend's name then jabbing her hockey stick into Rod's face, sending him stumbling backwards and falling into the filing cabinets behind him. The noise alerted Dave and I to the newly turned zombie's presence and my retro chain smoking friend was about to make sure that Rod's resurrection was a short one.

As Rod of the Dead moved towards Jonathon, Dave ran at him and booted him with force in the side of his head which sent him to the ground. But Dave wasn't finished yet. He opened the bottom filling cabinet drawer and emptied out its content. Grabbing Rod by the hair, he quickly forced his head into the open drawer then repeatedly slammed it shut. With the speed and ferocity in which he smashed Rod's head in the cabinet, it didn't take long for him to die, again. Dave wiped his blood soaked hands and face on the shirt of Rod and lit a cigarette.

"Take what you can, we're leaving," he said.

The road to my brother's house was uneventful compared to everything we had experienced up to this point. Apart from us, there was no 'living' activity on the streets. As we drove up Heath Road and Moughland Lane before turning onto Weston Road, we noticed many abandoned cars and several houses boarded up. These houses no doubt contained residents that had decided to stay put rather than attempt to flee and outrun the apocalypse. Unfortunately for the occupants, their houses had been surrounded by many of the undead and the numbers continued to grow. Zombie stragglers shuffling along the road would occasionally sniff the air intently, and then follow their decaying noses to where the fresh meat was hiding. Then there were the birds. Dead birds lay everywhere we looked. Starlings, pigeons, crows, magpies... come to think of it, I hadn't noticed any birds in the sky at all since those starlings dropped to their death outside the mayonnaise factory. Hang on a minute....

...That's better. I almost threw up in my mouth then. With everything that has been going on I had forgotten how much I hate the white gloopy devil condiment and accidentally thought about the stuff. Even writing the word triggers my gag reflex. Sorry about that. Back to death and destruction!

When Dave drove on to Weston Road the scale of the zombie outbreak became very apparent. It was now dusk and the tall houses to our left threw looming shadows on to the road. To our right was a low stone wall and behind that a sheer drop of almost 20ft down to allotments and Weston Point housing estate. Weston Road was a picturesque area of Runcorn and from its elevated position you could look out towards the neighbouring town of Widnes and further afield to Merseyside and the city of Liverpool. On a clear day, it was a beautiful view, just as long as you didn't look left or your eyes would be greeted by the biggest chemical plant and incinerator you had ever seen.

"Can you stop the car?" I asked Dave, who pulled the Thunderbird over to the side of the road.

We all left the vehicle, wanting to get a better look at the destruction caused by the outbreak. From our position we could see that the Silver Jubilee Bridge (or Runcorn Bridge if you're a local) had been almost destroyed. Something big, probably an airplane by the damage caused, had crashed through its middle, breaking the arch of the bridge and causing the Runcorn side to fall into the River Mersey. Only the Widnes half of the bridge now remained. Widnes itself was alight. Black smoke emitted from the flame engulfed housing estates of West Bank and beyond. Merseyside looked the same. Pockets of fire had broken out across the county making it look like the areas of Hale, Speke and Liverpool were communicating through smoke signals.

None of us uttered a word. What could be said that the view hadn't already told us? It confirmed that this thing was happening everywhere and not just contained to our own little corner of hell. You can't help but be filled with an overwhelming sense of doom when you're vision is filled with such destruction. A few minutes of this apocalyptic view was enough and we returned to the car. Dave drove for another two minutes to my brother's house which occupied a lowered position on Weston Road. Outside the house there was an old rusted gate in the small stone wall followed by steep steps which took you to the front door of the large detached property.

Dave parked the Thunderbird.

"There you go Ace, it might have taken us all day but we're here," Dave said.

"Do you think he's waiting for us Dad?" Emily asked.

"He better be. I've lost count of the amount of times we have discussed this very day. If I know my brother, he'll have been expecting us since this thing started. I wouldn't be surprised if he's pissed it took us this long to get here. Oh, and by the way, he won't be expecting anyone else but me and Emily so it's best if we go first. We don't need any more accidental deaths now do we?" I said with my eyes firmly fixed on Jonathon.

"I can't say I'm warming to your brother Ace. Are you sure he's ok? He doesn't exactly sound stable," Dave said.

"Don't worry Dave, as long as he sees me and Emily first everything will be fine. He's ok, really. As for stable? That one's up for debate," I said.

We began our walk down the long steep steps to my brother's house, overgrown weeds and bushes making visibility difficult in the quickly disappearing daylight. I led the way, followed by Emily, Dave and then the uncharacteristically quiet and sluggish Jonathon, the death of Rod playing heavily on his mind. Slowly we moved forward as I stiffly hobbled down the steps. I had swallowed several strong painkillers liberated from the medical centre and they had thankfully started to take effect, dulling the pain in my back to a bearable ache, but my movement was slow and every step towards the house brought us closer to an overpowering smell of death.

I could no longer move my legs no matter how hard I willed them to. All I had in this world was Emily and my brother and I feared something terrible had happened to Butty.

Dave walked past me, pushing aside the over grown shrubbery before disappearing down the remainder of the steps and into the undergrowth.

"Ace! You might want to come and look at this," he shouted through the vegetation.

Emily grabbed my arm and helped me forward as we joined Dave at the front of the house.

"You know you said whether your brother is sane or not is up for debate? Well I think now's the time for that debate lar," Dave said.

Every window to my brother's house appeared to be boarded up and nailed below every frame was an undead limb. Hands, feet, legs and arms all covered my brother's house. As if that wasn't disturbing enough, five wooden spikes had been hammered into the ground blocking his front door. On top of the spikes were the decaying rancid heads of zombies.

Butty was alive and he was a fucking genius!

I wandered to the side of my brother's house where he had constructed a make shift work station. A saw and an axe lay on blood stained and gut covered plastic sheets. This was obviously were my brother had cut up the zombies before nailing their chopped up body parts to the house. Oh, and placing their heads on spikes, let's not forget that! This was a brutal but brilliant idea. Butty had realised that what the zombies lacked in co-ordination, speed and brain power, they more than made up for with their sense of smell; I could see that now. The boarded up houses we had passed on our way here were surrounded by the living dead with more in the road, sniffing the air keenly before joining their flesh hungry brothers and sisters. My brother had figured this out and took steps to mask his own fleshy scent.

"Get fucked!"

"Who said that?" Dave asked, looking around to see where the aggressive voice came from.

"Get fucked!"

"Did you hear that? It's not just me is it? Someone is definitely telling us to get fucked?" Dave asked again.

"Yeah I heard it. I can't see anyone though," Jonathon replied.

"Get fucked!"

I knew who it was and so did Emily. Returning from the Devil's workshop I joined Dave and the others at the front of the house. Emily and I looked at each other and we both exchanged a massive smile.

"Butty! Open the bloody door will you? It's been a shitter of a day," I yelled.

"John?" my brother shouted.

Wooden panels broke away from a window on the first floor and my brothers face, completely covered in military camouflage make-up, peeped out.

"Where the fuck have you been and who the fuck have you brought with you?" my brother asked, obviously delighted to see me.

"Nice to see you too commando. This is my friend Dave and that's Jonathon, he's Emily's err, boyfriend," I explained.

"Ah yes, Jonathon. Nice to meet you finally," Butty said, offering Jonathon a thumbs up.

"Nice to meet you too Mr Diant," Jonathon replied.

"Fuck off with the Mr Diant will you. Call me Butty like every bastard else. Emily's told me so much about you I feel I know you already. How's things Emily love? Managed to keep your Dad alive I see." Butty said.

"You told your Uncle Butty about Jonathon but you couldn't tell me?" I asked Emily who replied by shrugging her shoulders.

Teenagers!

"Are you going to come down from there and open the door? It's freezing out here and I'm getting a little too familiar with the heads on these spikes," I said.

"No can do little brother. The whole ground floor is out of commission. You'll have to come to me," Butty said, lowering a rope ladder from the window.

Dave, Emily and then Jonathon climbed the rope ladder first. I wasn't looking forward to it in the slightest and was quite happy for everyone else to go before me. Heights were not my thing and even though the climb to my brother's window was only small, it still filled me with dread. Now it was my turn. I hate rope ladders. The way they swing when you climb, the way the rope dips when you place your foot on the step... everything!

"Come on John, get your arse into gear, you're letting a draft in here," Butty shouted down.

"Sod it," I thought to myself as I jumped on the rope ladder in an attempt to climb it as fast as I could, my thought being that if I did it quickly, I would be up there and through the window before my brain figured out I had left the ground. Bad idea! I got half way up and froze, petrified as the ladder started to sway back and forth. To make matters worse, my head was level with a zombie foot my brother had nailed to the wall and due to the rope ladder swinging, the foots rotting big toe kept prodding me in the forehead.

"Come on John, best foot forward!" my brother shouted. I looked up to see his big crazy grin peering back at me.

"You're not funny you know?" I said.

"I thought that was pretty good considering the circumstances. It's no small 'feet' climbing that ladder," Butty replied, struggling not to laugh through the remainder of his sentence.

Did I tell you how amusing my brother can be? No? Didn't think so.

I dug down deep and summoned the will to continue and I joined my brother and the others through the window. Once inside my brother quickly secured the window with more wood and nails.

We were stood inside what used to be a spare room, used mostly for storing my brother's enormous video collection.

It was still a storage room only instead of Butty's library of 1980s action films it was now wall to wall with tins of spam. Spam, spam, spam everywhere I turned.

"You know, I think it has been years since I last laid eyes on a tin of spam and now I know why. You've been stock piling them all." I said to my brother as he finished nailing the last plank of wood over the window.

"Well whilst everyone else has been sat at home watching Britain's Got The Kill Me Now Factor and tucking into their microwavable horse meat lasagnes I've been getting ready for the apocalypse haven't I? You would have known if you'd have picked up your bloody phone. I've been trying to call you for the last 5 days," my brother said.

"It was half term bruv, you know the score. Emily and me together for the whole week just father and daughter - no phone calls and no interference. But you could have texted me, I would have seen it or just called round." I explained.

"Don't do texting, my fingers are too fat. If I had tried to text you then what was meant to read 'John call me' would have come through as 'Jolly colander member' or something just as ridiculous. And I've been too busy preparing this place to go anywhere. I knew you'd come here anyway. I've been telling you for years that in the event of an apocalypse come to my house. I just thought you'd get here quicker that's all. Where have you been?" Butty asked.

269

"Well Dave and I were in work this morning when our boss tried to eat us. As soon we realised what was happening we picked Emily and Jonathon up from school and came here," I explained.

"Hang on a minute, you only realised what was going on this morning? I do wonder sometimes if we are actually related or if there was some kind of mix up at the hospital and mum and dad brought home the wrong baby. Don't you watch the news or go on the internet? There have been reports of a super plague spreading from Russia on every channel. Obviously the people turning into zombies bit was left out of the reports but it wasn't difficult to figure out. The governments of the world have been trying to keep it under wraps hoping they could contain it without causing a mass panic. Didn't work did it? I told you this day would come; I've been telling people for years. Everyone thought I was crazy but look at me now!" Butty said, his arms wide with a manic filled grin on his face.

"Butty, you're in full camouflage gear grinning like a Cheshire cat in a room surrounded by tins of spam, in a house that you've covered in zombie limbs. Whether you are crazy or not isn't in doubt," I replied.

"What's the deal with that by the way, the zombie parts?" Dave said, lighting another cigarette.

"Ah a fellow smoker! Dave it was wasn't it?" Butty said, extending his arm out for a handshake.

"That's right Ace, nice you meet you. Don't listen to John. It's not your fault if you're a bit of a wacko. It can't be easy growing up with him as your brother. I only work with him and I feel dumber for it. Fancy a smoke kidda?" Dave said, offering a cigarette to my brother.

Great, now I had two wise arses to deal with.

"I've got my own Dave. I could do with a light though if you don't mind," my brother said, opening a large walk in storage closet to reveal it completely chocker with cartons of cigarettes.

"Do you think you've got enough in there?" I said.

"Well I did until Dave here lit up and now I think we need more supplies," my brother replied.

"He's right Ace, there's not enough tabs in there for the two of us. They wouldn't last a week," Dave explained.

A week! There must have been thousands in there!

"Ciggy run in the morning Kidda?" Dave said to Butty.

"I know just the place," my brother replied, *"Now then where were we? Oh yes! Zombie limbs stuck to the house. They can smell you. I figured it out quite early on. Their eyesight isn't great and they have less co-ordination than a one legged blind dog but their sense of smell is second to none. So I managed to kill a few of the bastards, chop*

them up in my little work shop out the front then nail all the parts to the house. I've had no trouble since."

"Did you have to stick the heads on the spikes though? Seems a bit much if you just wanted to mask your smell," I asked.

"No, but you must admit it looks pretty awesome doesn't it? It's more to scare off any survivors really. I mean, would you try looting a house that looks like this?" my brother replied.

Like I said - genius! Mental of course, but the kind of mental this new world favours.

"It's getting late. Let me show you all what I've done with the place and fix you something to eat then you can get some rest," Butty said, ushering us out of the room and onto the hallway.

On the hallway it became quite evident why my brother couldn't open the door to his house and instead made us climb a rope ladder to the window. To my surprise, Butty had completely removed the stairway to the ground floor. You wouldn't think it to look at him but he's a clever bastard my brother. Should zombies enter the house they would have no way of reaching us in our elevated position.

"I took the stairs out a few days ago. You can still get down using the rope ladder. It attaches here on the hooks I've drilled into the bannister. I've locked up the cellar and

there's more food and water supplies in there should we need them. As you can see the electricity is still running so we have lights and hot water. But for how long is anyone's guess. I've got that covered though. There are two large generators in the cellar," Butty said.

"Where the hell did you find two generators?" I asked.

"I didn't find them little brother I've had them since the millennium. Don't forget I'm a seasoned doom mongerer. The end of the world just doesn't creep up on people like me. I've been planning for this my whole life. You know John, considering you're my brother you know very little about me," said Butty.

"To be honest Butty, you harp on about doomsday scenarios so often I tend to switch off. Every apocalypse conversation always ends the same way anyway, with you telling me that when Armageddon arrives, come to your house," I said.

"It's a good job you remembered the important part then, eh? Anyway, as I said there's hot water and I have plenty of towels so if anyone wants to freshen up you're more than welcome. Feel free to have a mooch around and I'll go and get some food on the go. I hope everyone likes spam?" Butty said, leaving the hallway and entering his bedroom which from where I was standing, looked to contain all of his kitchen utilities.

I have to admit that the spam was the best thing I'd had to eat in a long time. After we ate, we sat around the floor in my brother's room and for the first time all day we felt safe and able to relax. My brother even passed around a few beers which went down a storm. I even let Emily have one. Hey don't judge me; it's the end of the world! My brother said he had some stronger stuff brewing in the cellar but he's saving it for a special occasion. He's going to be waiting a long time that's all I can say.

It was after a few beers that my brother handed me an empty journal and said I should keep a record of our survival. He said keeping a journal could be vital for the future of the human race and when the war on the undead is finally over, it will be journals like mine that people will turn to, to understand what really happened. He said he was keeping one also but he wouldn't let me look at it in case I copied. Honestly, you'd think we were in school.

Now I don't know if this journal will help anyone and if you're reading this then well, you've just travelled along with me through the first day of the zombie apocalypse in my small part of hell called Runcorn.

Tomorrow? Well, tomorrow is another day but one thing is for sure - there will be no rest for the living.

The Gallery of the Dead

Darren Littler

Dawn Littler

Jo-Anne Burke & Anthony Rosenberg

Neil Gallagher

Nikki Mackie

Chris Mackie

Gina Noble

Andy Spokes

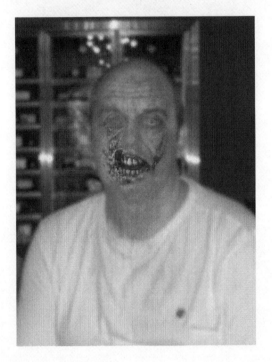

Mark Mckinlay

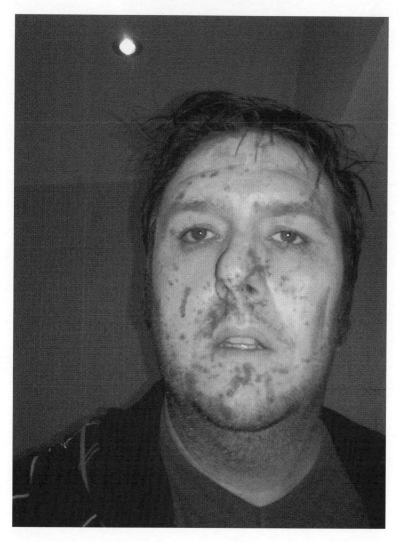

Francis Curran

Caitlin Williams

Printed in Great Britain
by Amazon.co.uk, Ltd.,
Marston Gate.